STORIES
UP TO A
POINT

STORIES
UP TO A
POINT

BETTE
PESETSKY

THE BODLEY HEAD
LONDON SYDNEY
TORONTO

'A Family History' originally appeared in *Cimarron Review* as 'Cliff Hangers: An Oral Family History,' and is reprinted here with the permission of the Board of Regents for Oklahoma State University, holders of the copyright.

'Care by Women' first appeared in *California Quarterly*. Magazine Copyright © 1978 by The Regents of the University of California.

Some of the other stories in this collection have been previously published in the following periodicals: *Beyond Baroque, Cottonwood Review, Kansas Quarterly, The Literary Review, The Ontario Review, Quarry West,* and *Wisconsin Review.*

British Library Cataloguing
in Publication Data
Pesetsky, Bette
Stories up to a point.
I. Title
813'.54[F]   PS3556.E733
ISBN 0-370-30483-7

Printed in Great Britain for
The Bodley Head Ltd
9 Bow Street, London WC2E 7AL
by Redwood Burn Ltd, Trowbridge
First published in Great Britain 1982

For Rose

I thank the National Endowment
for the Arts and the CAPS Program
of the New York State Council
on the Arts for their support
in the course of this work.

B.P.

CONTENTS

STORIES
UP TO A
POINT

MOE,
NAT, AND
∘ ∘ ∘ YRD ∘ ∘ ∘

I am a student of people who call on the telephone to voices who talk on the radio. There are two kinds of people who call. There are the people who call during the daytime hours. They believe in country and God and the immortality of the soul, whereas the ones at night believe in disputation and philosophy.

One day I decide to call. I dial the number and am put on hold. The man who answers is Moe. The subject tonight is dreams. I am an adept, for I dream in unison and also in quadraphony. Moe is interviewing a dream specialist. They're talking about REM sleep, about electrodes, about curious nocturnal behaviors. ·

Here's a dream for an expert.

My brother comes to the table. He says, I am going to become a priest. We look at him and we laugh. I have the calling, he says. But you are only eight years old, my mother says. I have the calling, he says.

Here's another one.

My father is standing on the roof. The slant is not steep,

so he has no trouble keeping his balance. Come down, Papa, we implore. He is irrational and in pain. He escaped through the bedroom window when we were supposed to be watching him. Now see what you have done, my mother scolds. Turn my back for an instant, and out he comes. Come down at once, she commands. You are in deep sedation. You are not yourself. He yields at once. Down on all fours, he crawls back to the window. Rationality appears with one rapid eye movement. He leaps to the street, dead on impact. His corpse exits far left.

Hold tires me, and I hang up and go to sleep.

It is ten a.m. I leave my desk, and I take a dime. I ride the elevator to the lobby. I go into a phone booth to dial the number. I am on hold for only a few seconds.

"I wish to talk about dreams," I say.

"What are you," Moe says, "a kook? Dreams were yesterday. Today is politics."

I do not have time to assemble my thoughts about politics. Moe disconnects me. Yet I am very political. I was active in the campaign of the other Shelley Winters. I worked in one of her storefront headquarters, where I folded papers and answered phones. I worked side-by-side with a man named Remal, who knew the real Shelley Winters. In time, I confessed to Remal the details of my divorce and its attendant pain. One evening, after headquarters closed, Remal took me to a party in honor of Shelley Winters. It was a crowded party. Remal introduced me to Shelley Winters' accountant's brother, who shook my hand and squeezed my shoulders.

I like you very much, he said.

I eat dinner at six, help my daughter with her homework, and go to a revival of *Mr. Deeds Goes to Washington.* At eleven p.m., I turn on the radio. They are interviewing someone who is very upset about how people are abandoning the church.

I dial the number, which I have memorized. The line is busy. I hang up and dial again. Listen, Moe, I compose in my mind. Many people are reentering the religious life. My brother, for instance, left the seminary. He went out into the world, which had changed a lot in five years. His father was now dead. His mother had moved to California. He went out into the world, and he shacked up with a girl named Leonida. They became speed freaks, and she had a baby who died. Three times I dug into child-support money and gave them for food. My brother has reentered the religious life. He sent me his blessing and his belief that he is a finer person now.

The phone connects. "Hi, Moe," I say.

"You!" he screams and hangs up.

○ ○
○

In the passage of time, which is five years, I remarry, my daughter turns sixteen, and my husband enters into what he claims is his last malaise. I have continued to listen to the radio voices. Thematically and contextually, it is as before. The man I listen to is named Nat.

Nat has a sexual expert tonight. But my new husband keeps coughing and lies awake. Calling is out of the question. It is dangerous to walk the streets at night or I would go to the phone booth on the next corner. Nat, I say inside my head, I have taken a lover, Nat. I know that this is not unusual, but five years ago I would not have done this. You know how it is, Nat. Cultural things change.

I listen, but no one is saying what I would say. They are talking about kisses, about positions, about making it in and out of marriage.

My lover and I meet when convenient. We follow no particular routine. We are not every Thursday or that kind of thing.

My mother has a lover in California. But my father, of course, is dead.

One day, my daughter, who has been carefully trained, comes to the dinner table. I am going to enter a convent, she says. My husband, her stepfather, says, That is absurd. All over the world young women are stepping back into the world from the Dark Ages. Nevertheless, my daughter says, I will enter a contemplative order.

I risk certain death or maiming and walk to the phone booth. With Nat, you can mention anything. I dial the number. I have a roll of dimes. The hold is not long. Maybe because the crazies are all out on dates.

"Hi there," says Nat. "Have you called for our survey? Do you still smoke?"

"No," I say, not wishing to antagonize. "Never."

"Chalk up another no-no," says Nat.

"Can I talk about religion?" I say. "Or dreams or politics? How about sex stuff?"

"Talk away, baby," he says. "Ticky-ticky."

"Religion," I say. "I do not know whether it is just bunk or for real. I mean in the darkness of your soul, aren't you alone, as Kierkegaard says?"

"Any way you want it," says Nat.

"Actually, I smoke," I say.

I pocket my dimes and go back to the apartment. I take my husband to the doctor, where he is X-rayed, bled, and sampled.

He is fine, the doctor says. It is an affliction of the mind. My husband shakes his head. They are at cross-purposes, the doctor and my husband.

I take my husband home, where he remains. He is convinced that he will die. I feed him and tend to his needs.

In the spring, the opinion of the doctor changes. My husband is ill. He is terminal. My husband turns to me triumphant. See? he says.

My daughter leaves the convent. She turns butch and lives with a girl named Stephania. She is arrested for indecent exposure on the Boston Common. I post her bail. She disappears. My husband cannot console me. What kind of consolation can you get from the dying?

I dial Nat. "What becomes of the families of the children who are lost in the world?"

"Come again, baby?"

"I mean, is there meaning in this for me? Am I looking in the right place?"

"Tally-ho!" says Nat, disconnecting.

My husband begs me to remarry when he is gone. Three times I tell him it is ridiculous. It is not the custom in my family. You will be alone, my husband declares. Who will know if you get home safely at night? Who will check your tax returns for careless errors? Your mind is wandering, I weep, and hold his wasted body.

When my husband dies, I am not home. I am passing out pamphlets for environmental purity as part of my community responsibility. I have never planned a funeral before. More than a hundred people attend. I had a popular husband.

Alone in my apartment, I carry out the regular functions. I receive a letter from my daughter, who has had an apocalyptic experience that has cleansed her soul. She is returning to the church. She will enter a far stricter order. She will be totally sequestered.

Nat is interviewing an astrologer. I dial him, am put on hold, eat a cheese sandwich while waiting.

"I have these dreams," I say at last, "where my brother and daughter become members of a religious community with faces hidden by cowls. My father and husband are in their graves."

"You are a deeply pessimistic person," says the astrologer. "You are a Capricorn, perhaps?"

"Scorpio," I say. "I am aggressive and pushy, especially around Christmastime."

"These dreams," the astrologer says, ignoring my outburst, "reveal your search for the meaning of existence."

"Says who?" I say, and hang up.

In time things happen to me over which I have no control. I write to my daughter, my brother, even to California, where my mother lives. From my daughter, who is sequestered, I never hear. My brother sends me a religious picture, a pamphlet, and the knowledge that he is one with me in my grief. My mother writes on the back of a postcard with a La Jolla sunset. She writes in a tiny, spidery hand. The weather is fine, she says. It will pass, she says. This is how the newly-bereaved behave.

Joe interviews a man who is eighty-seven. The man is in the throes of a vigorous life. He owes it all to hobbies. Recently, he has begun to make collage pictures from candy wrappers. Listeners are urged to send him their old candy wrappers.

The hell with Joe. Nat and Moe were closer to things.

Among my complaints are migraines, loss of libido, compulsive reading of the New York *Post*. Gradually, however, I regather myself, and am elected co-chairperson of the local community-planning board. I participate in demonstrations for many new causes. In the rotogravure section of the Sunday newspaper there is a picture of me at the forefront of an exceptionally heterogeneous group of demonstrators. I am the woman with wild hair and waving fists. I am shown shouting at someone.

I coin quotable phrases, like "the defrocked of society," and become an expert on saving landmarks, schools, and neighborhoods. But there is still a loss in me, a yearning, an incompleteness. I can find no peace with either Nat or Moe. I switch to Yrd. Yrd is into philosophies and deeper meanings.

Soon after I appear in the rotogravure, I am asked to be interviewed in the two a.m. slot. I can choose among Joe, Moe, Nat, or Yrd, that's how much radio wants me. Basing my decision on spiritual kinship, I choose Yrd. Taking no chances, I do my hair, my nails.

Yrd squints at me. "You do not look like the lady in the picture."

"True," I say. "I was distilled in a moment of grief."

Yrd and I discuss the meaning of community involvement and the modern woman.

In answer to a question, I say, "I do not see it as an opportunity to escape from the kitchen. I see it, rather, as a chance to become an integral part of history."

"Do you feel deeply about your causes?"

"I feel the importance of continuity."

Yrd takes a call. "I wish to talk about reincarnation," says the voice.

Yrd turns to me, and I nod. I will carry the ball. "Reincarnation," I say, repeating the word to formulate my thoughts. "Reincarnation is not necessarily the rebirth of the person. Reincarnation can be conceived as a repetition of manifestations of a culture. A reincarnation of patterns."

Yrd picks it up from there with Indian lore and Bridey Murphy and some very good stuff on Sufi. After the show, we use his telephone to call his wife and then hang up when she starts in with her dreams.

○ ○ ○

FAMILY
ROMANCES

There has suddenly appeared in my city a surplus of babies
born with hydrocephalus, atresia of the foramen of Magendie,
cerebral neoplasms, cranium bifidum, and other chromosomal
aberrations. Thus, I have dark thoughts of incest, of syphilis,
of genes gone mad. I wonder too if when these infants grow
up, they will press upon us in the streets, causing panic, a rise
in Nietzscheism, and a profit to the American Nazi Party.
Shifton, however, laughs. This has always been with us, he
says. Someone will take care of it.

I am, of course, much changed since the original appearance of my secret, which is a secret that has evolved from
period to period. At first, it dealt with sex and its manifestations—namely, with desire, longing, passion, being found out.
This secret later became depression and symptoms of anxiety
—namely, rootlessness, alienation, possibility of failure on a
colossal and overwhelming scale.

We have my scene with the old woman.

The old woman is very upset when the new management
company asks her for a security deposit. I have lived here for

twenty-five years, she says. And now they don't trust me. Twenty-five years.

How could I tell her that all that time in an apartment building counted for nothing?

Before my family left Wisconsin, they were renters. True renters are a species apart. They don't put up anything that can't be taken away. Still, we belonged there and made an opera of good-byes. We're coming back, we swore. We'll write. Take care of the plants.

I met the old woman as I headed for the incinerator. Leaving, I hear, she says scornfully. For ten years we had been neighbors. She was a good neighbor and watched my apartment when I traveled. Yes, I answer, trying to look sad. I couldn't wait to leave. I guess you're looking for somewhere newer, she says. It won't be as good, mark my words. Walls like tissue in those places, skinny little rooms. I know, I know, I say, swinging my garbage pail. I also say, But you must realize I've gotten a divorce. Now I must move because I need better transportation. The old woman squints at me. You don't look too good, she says. If you want, drop in for tea. You must be lonely. Loneliness is something I could write a book about.

She makes me shiver. I take my one child and flee.

After Wisconsin, we lived eight years on Coconut Hill and six years on Palm Road. My mother slammed that door with satisfaction. "Thank God. I don't ever want to see the inside of another little house," she says. She divorced my father in the spring. We talked her out of doing it in the winter, thinking when the snow melted she would change her mind. She didn't. My father married my mother's younger sister, Aunt Margerie Wales, and bought a house on Quelling Knoll. We never saw him again.

One day I drove to the city. I stood in a doorway across from the building where my mother lived. She has given up politics and religion. She is trying to be aware and modern. She has given up crying. She is into macramé and assorted crafts. I follow her for three hours. She goes into the places where mothers go.

My mother did not speak badly of my father. So my sister and I were forced to eavesdrop and to pry. Here is a scene my sister related to me. It happened before our parents parted.

"It's a damn shame," he says, "seeing you so nasty, so sour. We haven't lived together as man and wife for two years, but we've been civil to each other, Marietta, and we've been civilized. Now you act like I'm a fiend, a Bluebeard, a Jack the Ripper."

"Another woman wouldn't mean a thing to me. Not a thing. But this—this is like incest," my mother says.

"Margerie Wales is your sister. She is not my daughter."

"I cannot be civilized about this," my mother says.

"Then," he says, glowering, "I won't be either." My father looks around the room for something suitable. He decides upon a large pot of ivy and flings it to the floor.

She flinches. "How could you! The ivy!" She sinks to her knees on the red carpet and stares at the plant shattered in front of her, pot broken, roots exposed. "I raised that for six years." My mother moans, she croons, she grieves. "It was like a child."

My father is pleased. "There!" he says in triumph. "*There* is an indecent relationship. You and any plant!" He waves his arms wildly. Containers with plants are everywhere.

She grabs a chair, holds it in front of her as would a lion-tamer. "Don't you dare touch another!"

My sister's name is Winnetka. She married a widower. They have two children. We are very fond of each other. Yet, when I look at her strange face, I cannot really remember that we shared the same house, the same thoughts, the same parents. I have let Winnetka take the furniture from our parents' home. It will give her children a heritage, I believe. I have faith in objects. They are always there.

Once there was a terrible snowstorm in Wisconsin. We couldn't leave the house on Laguna Drive. There was a sale at the store where my mother worked. My mother stood at the window, regretting the lost commissions. My father nuzzled her neck. "We are alone," he says. "Alone in this world of whiteness. All the world is gone."

"Alone," my mother says. "Ah, yes, alone. Just you and me and our two daughters and the dog."

The factory at Racine closed. We had to move from Wisconsin.

"Just as well," my father says. "All things have a purpose."

"Purpose," my mother says.

"You'll see," my father says.

We will now test his theory that bad luck is geography. We leave our home—and just in case it might help, we add an *e* to the end of our name. We go to New York and stay in the house that Aunt Margerie Wales owns. My father was right; his luck changed.

You are seeking a neurotic dependency relationship, my first husband tells me. Your interpersonal relations are flawed and your ability to interface. You cannot rationalize your father's marriage. Nuts, I say. You never met him. Or her. You do not even know Aunt Margerie Wales. I could, he says. You could call them. I am not curious, I say. I know them.

"How terrible for your mother," another husband says. "And for you. Did you know that they were lovers? Your father and your aunt?"

"It wasn't a blood relationship," I say, and then, "Why did you marry me? For exotic relatives? If so, let me tell you about my cousin Lenore, who may or may not have been an hermaphrodite. Do you want to hear about her?"

"Very funny," the other husband says.

I am in my car, and I am driving through the city from east to west. There is a woman standing in her back yard burning trash in a wire basket. She stares at nothing. The wind whips her robe around her body. So why am I staring at her?

My father brings me a large rubber doll. It is shaped like a baby. The whispering voices tell me that it is very expensive. Dope, my mother says. How about shoes? How about a coat? Yet my mother makes a large bow of blue ribbon. For me or for the doll? Who remembers?

Blue is your color, my husband says. All right, so blue is my color. He takes me for a ride. It takes me a while to figure out where we are going. Turn around, I shout. I called them, he says. They are waiting. He sounds like an old man. No, I say. No, I scream.

Secrets cannot be kept. They show up in last wills and testaments, in the malevolent words of the dying. In time, all secrets are revealed and enter the public domain. Secrets about hemophiliacs, revolutions, heresies, disastrous rental agreements.

My Uncle Leon left his wife. They must have been in their mid-forties at the time and married more than twenty years. My

Aunt Beulah was a short woman from Cracow. She had a thick body and always wore brown lisle stockings and a black dress. Uncle Leon was also a short person. He came from a village some distance from Cracow. He was a rural boy. He was seven years old when he came to this country. She was ten. He left her in the classical way. The family moaned and tore their hair. I saw my Aunt Beulah beat her breasts with a soup ladle.

"Tell me," I asked, "do you miss him so much?"

"The stars," Aunt Beulah declared. "The moon. He is the silver ash in the fields, the poetry of Mickiewicz." She dropped to her knees and would have smashed her head against the linoleum except I threw my arms around her.

"I'll die too," I swore. "I'll hold my breath until I die too."

Much later Aunt Beulah became fifty-eight and my political mentor, and I became a young woman who was picking her up to take her to a rally. When I rang the doorbell, Aunt Beulah opened the door. Her cheeks were red. Her forehead glistened. "Darling," she whispers. "He is back. My Leon has returned from the West."

"Throw him out!" I shout. "Get rid of him."

"Hush." She is very stern. "He is ill. A tumor. He's got a tumor inside him."

"So he comes to you," I say. "Ask yourself why."

"You know nothing about love," she says. "If you cannot speak kindly of Leon, do not come back."

I go to the rally alone. But socialism without Aunt Beulah is not so thrilling.

I'll tell you why I have six children. This is a conversation with my mother.

"No one has six children," she says.

"People have six children," I answer. "Even seven."

"Name anyone we know," she says. "It's too many grand-children. Who can even remember so many names?"

"Next time you come," I say, "I will hide four of them in a closet."

My mother opens her purse. "Have you enough money? Are the support checks on time?"

There is a commotion in the back of the apartment. Mar-lena, who is fourteen, is fighting with her brother Edward, who is twelve. She is calling him a son of a bitch, and he is calling her words whose meaning I don't understand. I race into the room. My hand shoots out in a fury of passion or the other way around. I slap their faces.

"Why did I have so many children?" I shout.

"Why did you have so many children?" they shout.

Aunt Margerie Wales sends a letter. My father has cancer, but he is not dying fast. He is a very old man and that is sparing him, since within the old nothing grows quickly. I fight with my son Arnold and my daughter Lita. They do not want to visit him. They say that the room he is in will smell and will be too dark. My aunt pushes them toward the bed. "Kiss, kiss," she says.

On Tuesday, I have an appointment to see Andrew. I want a loan. I have bills, clothes, dentists, tuition. Three of the children are his.

Aunt Margerie Wales is not a pretty woman. She was named after her father, who was a farmer and died, leaving nothing from his life of labor. Margerie Wales is a plump, dark-haired woman who worked hard and saved her money until she owned a four-family house, which she kept in perfect condition. She believed in hard work. My mother is slender and sharp-tongued and not successful.

When we lived in my aunt's house, she always said things to my mother, things like, "Let him be, Marietta. Let the man live."

"Mind your business," my mother would say. "You don't know. All this talk about luck. He's got a good position now. Fortune is smiling."

Aunt Margerie Wales blinks with her blue eyes. They are her best feature. You are a nice child, she says to me. I pity you. It is better to be like Winnetka and see clearly.

I love you, I say.

We could stay here forever, I decide in my heart. Here forever in this orderly house with Aunt Margerie Wales. But my father becomes successful, and so we move to a house of our own on Coconut Hill, where I grow up and don't hug people so much.

Winnetka swears she remembers seeing my father kiss my Aunt Margerie Wales. So what? I say. People are always kissing. Don't be a jerk, Winnetka says. You know what I mean. Stay out of my way! our mother shouts at us.

This is a scene, I think.

"I love you," my father says. "You are gentle and sweet."

"I love also," Margerie Wales says.

They have no thoughts about anyone else. How clearly I see them. He is an aging man, pale from indoor lights. She is not pretty.

"I've had an absolutely great time," I say. "I mean, I have six children, and I live in Manhattan. There were three husbands, and it never worked out. The fault is mine."

In the afternoon, when I took the baby for a walk in his carriage, I wore ankle socks. He hated that, one of the husbands. He told me a million times how he hated that. Wear anything, that husband said. Wear jeans like the other women. Just don't wear those socks.

From one to two, I say, I read poetry. I never do anything else. It doesn't matter, he says, staring in horror at the debris of someone's paper and paints. What doesn't matter? I say. I'm warning you, he says. Don't wear them.

I'd cleaned up the place. I'd ironed my blue wash-and-wear. Blue is my color. The dinner was Cordon Bleu. The children seemed positively governessed. He came in waving a letter. "Was it too much to ask for you to have mailed the gas and electric bill? Too much?"

Where in my genes was it patterned that I was destined to remember to mail checks? Where was it decided that I would be a mailer? I threw my glass at him. It was water that went all over his face and onto the lapels of his jacket. So why couldn't it have been grape juice?

I have become one of the exotic relations. I had three husbands. There were six children. I heard one of my nieces say that I was an animal. A breeder. And it wasn't even a matter of faith. Faith? Who's she kidding?

Albert, my third husband, has taken to calling me up evenings. "It's me," he says. "We have just come out of a nice Mexican restaurant on Broadway. I had guacamole, chicken mole, chalupas, and a mango frappe. Presently, we shall walk downtown. The night is rich with promise. In the Eighties, we shall stop at that little bakery I know and have espresso and rum cakes."

"Albert," I say, "enjoy yourself."

"See what you are missing, my pequeña?" he says. "My schöne Seele, my little darling?"

If only he would call earlier when the children are awake.

They would run for the phone. Let him tell them about Szechuan dumplings in hot oil, a nude happening, a storefront theater piece celebrating the hopelessness of everything.

"Are you a Margaret Sanger dropout?" Shifton, my new
friend, asks.

"Who's that?" I reply.

Mrs. Cazzio has a man friend who comes on Tuesdays and
Thursdays about ten in the morning. He is a moderately obese
man, and I do not see him as a lover. Still, she looks happy
these days, and the appearance of her skin is smooth and
flushed. One Tuesday, I saw her wait in the lobby with a light
coat over her dress. Her daughter Galena was home with a
cold. So Mrs. Cazzio waited in the lobby near the door and then
made semaphore signals with her hands. The blue car drove
away.

All the things that happen to everybody will someday happen to my children.

T H E
T H E O R Y
○ O F   S E T S   ○

These old clippings say that my mother was an anarchist. Don't
believe it. What's the evidence? A few photographs taken at
rallies with those men from the West Coast? Was it her manner? The forcefulness and the pounding fist? They described
her as "beefy," a cruel word to apply to a woman. My mother's
friends used to gather in our kitchen. Anarchists? Revolution-
aries? They were just noisy people. They couldn't keep a secret
on a bet. Sometimes, when my father wasn't around, they
would wonder why my mother married him. Not a unionist, a
money-grubber. Someone would see me and say, *"Stille, das
Kind."*

I was a backward child, shy. Mostly, they ignored me. Then
one day I was to go to school. My mother dressed me in a
jumper and white stockings. I went away from the kitchen, and
everyone wished me luck.

As I started out, there was a familiar laryngeal tightening
and a pain from intercostal muscles. Later, they would link this
to my mother's being a silver-voiced orator at union meetings
and to my father, a liquid-voweled salesman.

Say hello, my mother called to me as I walked through the gates. Step right up there, she insisted. Speak out, be friendly.

Was there a spell on me?

The child is too much alone, my mother said.

She did not enroll me in the parish school to be lost among dozens. I was sent to the smaller academy with higher monthly payments.

We'll find the money, my mother said.

She believed in disciplined education. It had nothing to do with religion.

The nuns liked me. I was one of the quiet ones with a gold star for behavior. I became part of the group made up of Kay Preddy, Priscilla Weeks, Louise Urslane, Margaret Chase. We all lived within walking distance. We were the plain ones who sat in the back and trembled when noticed.

In our last year in school, Kay Preddy's uncle, a jeweler, got us five small gold lockets with a tiny ruby centered in each heart. On the back of each he engraved the numeral 5.

It took us three months to save from our allowances the six dollars each locket cost. We had a ceremony and swore to be together forever as we clasped the lockets around each other's throats. We were all going to St. Clare's or St. Gabriel's or someplace like that.

o o
o

Bankruptcy, my father said. If it rains, who does it rain on? he said right after that.

He was a good man. Nothing had happened to my brother and me when our mother died. We didn't go to the relatives. My father did not start drinking or any of the things predicted.

But his business, after years of giving orders, wasn't his any more. He stormed through our flat cursing that God, who did not exist, was against him. My days at St. Clare's or at St. Gabriel's were out of the question. He would not hear of it. God and I were to part. What could I do? Trembling, I told the girls, and together we prayed.

Meanwhile, I was enrolled in the local high school. The students seemed wild and different. But after a few weeks, I fell in with the journalism crowd and ate with Ellen Brenwick, Nora Venn, Elsie Kale—and two boys, Bill Robbins and Isaac Tilberg. With the money I had, I bought a skirt and blouse like Nora's.

On Friday evenings, the journalism crowd met at Nora's house. Her mother was a widow and was pleased with our company. We sat in the kitchen, popped corn, and ate hamburgers. We spoke about the world. We were the journalism crowd.

In my senior year, I won a state scholarship. My father was remarried that spring to a Mrs. Melton, a widow. She was a nice woman, middle-aged and childless. I didn't fit in any more. I was glad to be going away.

My father drove me to college in the '53 Chevy. We rode for five hours before we reached the university. Together, we carried my trunk up to my room. Good-bye, I said. We shook hands. My father cleared his throat. Baby, he said, the thing is this. We are going to Florida. Mrs. Melton thinks that we should buy into her brother's gas station and diner.

I squeezed his hand. I understood.

Well, he said, we are going like the first of October. You'll be all right?

My roommate was Anne Arthur. We had been paired by com-
puter. She was a blonde from Buffalo.

Hello, I said. Hello back, she said.

I unpacked my clothes.

Anne and I went to Orientation with two other girls on our
floor, Michelle Hall and Adie Despotis. At a get-acquainted
dance, I met Jack Wargrave. We began to date. I got a letter
from my father. He wished me lots of luck. The stuff left
behind in my room in the apartment had been packed into
cardboard cartons. Mrs. Polodin next door had offered to store
them in her attic, he wrote. What was left? Children's books,
old uniforms, junk. If I never saw any of it again, that was all
right.

I began dating Melvin Abrahams, Ronald Skinner, Myron
Brewster, and Joel Thomas. Anne and I took three classes
together. We were both virgins. One night I slept with Jack.
I confided in Anne.

On a winter afternoon crossing the campus, I saw Louise
Urslane. Later, when we happened to meet, we stared past each
other. In my sophomore year, Nora Venn transferred to the
university. We ate lunch together once.

I love it here, she said. We could share a room next year.

I nodded, not to hurt her feelings.

Anne Arthur was okay with me.

Anne and I drove down to Florida with Michelle, Adie,
Ronald, Jack, Myron, and Joel. We went to Ft. Lauderdale. My
father and Mrs. Melton lived in Tarpon Springs. I didn't see
them, although I did send a card.

After graduation, I went back to the city and got a job. I shared an apartment with Michelle. She took me to a party given by some people from her office. Isaac Tilberg was one of them.

I said, For goodness sakes. He said, You haven't changed.

○ ○
○

Isaac and I decided to get married. We had a civil ceremony. Michelle was my attendant. Afterwards, we had a small reception. Nora, Myron, Bill, and Adie were invited. Ronald brought his new bride, Lydia.

Isaac could make money.

We are making money, he said.

When we moved, it was to a five-room apartment in a midtown building. As in most new buildings, nothing worked right. We formed a tenants' association. We had a cocktail party for some of the people we met. There were Bill and Susie Flynn, Annabel and Arthur Rexine, Ms. Toni Meadows, Pete Sarkin, and the Blenfords. Ronald and Lydia moved into the building. Ronald and Isaac were cooking up deals. There were many parties. We did the apartment in brown and white.

During our second year in the building, Annabel got pregnant, and the Rexines moved to the Island. Pete took up with someone and vanished. Bill and Susie stayed until their baby was one year old. Then Susie got pregnant again, so they left. I came home one day and found Isaac on the living-room floor with Nora.

I rented a one-room place. I didn't take anything with me. I bought new from discount stores. I used madras throws over everything and ate badly. I thought more about things and started taking graduate courses at night school. After classes I'd go for coffee with Cindy Coppings, Rose Heath, Beryl Lily, Alex Brin, Mrs. Collins, and Ray Gunther. We were older and tired. We all worked days.

This was my life for maybe eight, ten months. Then one Saturday I met Lydia on a crosstown bus. We went to a bar for some drinks. I'm divorced now, she said. Yes, I said. I think I'm getting one too. Lydia stared at me. She said, I will get you a lawyer. It is madness not to. Anyway, I am glad to see you. I always liked you.

Lydia took me back to her apartment. I got it all, she said. Ronald got some broad and that's all he got. She said, Move in here. There is room enough. We can keep each other company when the world gets rough.

I left everything behind—the madras throws, the sharptined forks. I moved in. Lydia's lawyer took my case. I hardly ever saw Lydia. She was always out. But later we gave some parties. Toni Meadows came, and Bill and Susie Flynn, Dominic Rutkin, Basil Humbolt, Winston Xavier, Dora Lace, and Laurence Totter. Then we gave some more parties. Different people came.

THE
PASSING
○ ○ PARADE ○ ○

I work in the suburbs. Why? he asked me. He was not a lover of nature. It takes me twenty minutes, I tell him, from kitchen to office. An industrial park in an army of maples. A factory in an ocean of grass. How could I leave? Fall was beautiful. Winter banked the driveways with snow. Forget it, he said. Take the job in the city.

I could leave? The decision was reversible. All coins turn, my mother once said. Adapt.

I became a commuter. It wasn't difficult. I bought a new alarm clock. I got up an hour earlier to catch the train. I didn't really mind being a commuter—although in the past when I rode the train to the city, it was only to go to an event. The city was never someplace I went every day.

In the mornings, crossing Grand Central Station from track to exit, I was often bumped. Sharpened elbows plunged into me, attaché cases assaulted my thighs, bodies reared into mine. I tried to apologize. I'm sorry, I'm sorry. Did they hear? No one ever replied. They just moved past me. Sometimes they looked at their watches. My feelings were hurt.

I could not believe what I witnessed. My fault? I adapted.

For me the most convenient exit was to Lexington Avenue, which was the permanent station of two crazies. One was a fat old woman who wore layers of clothing. Cotton, wool, linen. Black, red, yellow. Pieces of forgotten sweaters now and then erupted from beneath the edges of a gray coat. A man's coat, I think. The woman had a harsh voice. She yelled, "Hey! Get me a doctah! Get me a doctah!" We all walked past her. Some hurried as they neared her, fearing contagion. The woman was there every day. The other crazy was a man in his forties. He owned dirty suits and changed them in accord with some rigorous sequence. Daily, he waved his hands and exhorted us in an inflected glossolalia. "Dmare aga ya!" he shouted. "Dmare yato!" In very cold weather, he vanished.

I thought that these were the only Lexington Avenue exit crazies. But one morning I paused near a bank of phone booths to unfold my rain scarf. The woman standing near me was white-haired and sensibly dressed. "Stupid!" she shouted at me. "What do you think you're doing? My granddaughter wouldn't do that!" With folded scarf, I ran for the doors.

Walking to my office, I saw a tall man with stiff black hair that turned to curls down his neck. He wore a suit and carried a raincoat and a briefcase. He moved quickly. I couldn't keep up. Why was I trying? His left shoulder hit the tail of a woman's braid and whipped it across her face. The shield of his briefcase made a path through the people who crossed the sidewalk and came toward him. He was gone before I could call out. The reason for my hesitation? Uncertainty. I thought he was my brother Edward. He looked like Edward. Edward's office was in the vicinity.

I have recently discovered that the backs of people look

more familiar than the faces. "Violet," I say. The woman turns.
"Sorry, sorry," I apologize as I stagger away. Yet the hair, the
set of the shoulders, the walk were Violet's.

Maybe it really was Violet.

My daughter mocks this inclination of mine. From the
back, the average person, she says, looks like anyone. If you
want to be distinctive from the back, you have to have a hump.

On very cold days, an old neuralgia bothers me with fresh
arrows of pain running from cheek to forehead. I wrap my face
bandage-like with a woolen scarf. I am not self-conscious. From
the front, everyone is a stranger to me. Who will know? I wait
for the bus. I queue up along with everyone else. But before
the bus comes, late arrivals cut into the line in front of me.
Only once do I protest—a man in a heavy quilted coat. His
fingers take me by the throat. "I'll call a cop," I whisper. "Wait
your turn," the man says, "or I'll bust you one."

Looking out the bus window, I thought I saw Potter hurry-
ing across the street. Wasn't it Potter? The man carrying a
shopping bag with a long, skinny bread sticking out over the
top? The bread was the clincher. Potter loved bread. He was
always buying different varieties of bread. I had been married
to Potter, but I hadn't seen him since we separated twenty
years ago. It was Potter. I wasn't wrong. Potter was headed for
a small red car illegally parked. I saw him take the ticket off
the windshield and throw it into the street.

I often baked bread for Potter. I even learned to make
skillet bread on a camp stove. I made it once on a camping trip
to Lake Mead. Lake Mead was very hot in summer. Twenty
years ago camping was an adventure. The campground was full
of people in canvas tents. Two sites away from us there was
a pickup truck. There was an old man, an old woman, three

children. There was no tent, just the truck. From Las Vegas, the old woman said. Is that where they lived or where they were running from? The old man drank. He and the old woman had loud quarrels. One day someone's camp stove vanished. At that time, thefts from campgrounds were unheard of. It might have been the beginning of the Modern Period.

Mornings, the children woke us up with their yelling. One morning the old woman was making breakfast. There was one egg and a frankfurter to be divided three ways. The children were screaming that it wasn't enough. That afternoon, either because the old man had trouble with the rangers or ran out of whiskey, the pickup truck pulled away.

Someone actually stole my morning newspaper. One minute it was tucked under my arm while I was opening my purse for change. The next minute someone had snatched it away. How could I accuse anyone? Everybody around me had a newspaper.

At a concert in a college auditorium in mid-Manhattan, I mentioned the stolen newspaper to my friend Gertie Vodel. "Ripped from my hands," I said.

She nodded and clutched her purse tighter.

Gertie Vodel pointed out a couple to me during intermission. "Charles and Sophie," she whispered. As Charles and Sophie moved up the aisle, I could see that Charles limped.

"He was in a terrible accident last year," Gertie Vodel said.

"Really?" I said.

"While he was in the hospital, Sophie left him. Their daughter flew in from Duluth. She was hysterical and sobbed, 'Mother, Mother, how could you?' Charles was in traction for his neck. There was internal bleeding, serious doubt he would walk again. And Sophie just left him. No one could believe it.

So his daughter had to go back to her children, her husband. Then after five months Sophie returned. Charles was just out of the hospital. He had a live-in nurse."

"And?"

"Not a word," Gertie Vodel said. "Never one word of explanation."

We turned to stare at the backs of the couple. She wore a peculiar dress. From where I was looking, it looked peculiar.

I have discovered the midtown reference library. I search through the reference books on the fourth floor. Accidentally, I find facts. So Eliot did not graduate from the school he claims he graduated from. I find in the library addresses of firms that I am interested in locating. I jot down this information on scraps of paper. I find out how old people are.

On the street I join a man who is trying to lift an old lady who has fallen down. The woman is not heavy. Like she's a cloud, the man says. On the count of three, we bend over to grab her old arms. Upsy-daisy, the man says. I need a lawyer, the old lady says. A bus knocked me down.

I saw no bus.

As I hurry away, the old lady yells, Give me your name! Give me your name!

All the young girls who walk by have long straight hair parted in the middle. Everybody's hair is brown. It is enough to make you believe in mutations.

My daughter Abby has long straight hair parted in the middle, and it's brown. If she were walking with those girls, would I recognize her? She could be with them right now and I'm missing her. She lives in a dormitory somewhere in the city. Suddenly, the girls rush forward, engulfing an old man in a flood of hair and then passing on. They are running to catch a crosstown bus that will maybe smash into a little red car. A long skinny bread will break in half.

My hair is black. Stephen, Abby's father's the same.

Lally, Edward's wife, calls me at the office to make a luncheon date. I have only an hour, I tell her, and then I must be back at work. Lally agrees. Yes, she says, of course. At the restaurant where we have lunch, I drink two glasses of wine. I get drunk on one glass. Lally's conversation is about her children. So I bring up Abby's accomplishments. But I don't mention the mutated hair.

For the spring holiday, Abby plans to go to California to be with her father, although I have heard that Stephen has already returned to the city. Edward says he has. Edward is Stephen's lawyer.

After work I go to a bar with three people from my office. One drink, I tell them. They all live on the Upper West Side. There isn't anyone in our office who doesn't live on the Upper West Side. Except me, of course. Trains, trains, someone says. How long does it take you to get to the city? I tell them forty minutes. A man whistles. It takes me that long to get a hard-on, he says.

I am thinking of moving to the city. Edward is always after me to move to the city. If you owned a house, he says, I could understand staying in the sticks. Roots. But one apartment is like another.

Abby insists that her schedule does not permit her to meet me for lunch. And she hates the suburbs. Might as well live in the North Woods, she says. Everything is in the city.

My lawyer calls me at the office. Arnold may come back to the city too, he says, and if he does, we can hit him with all our guns. I don't tell Edward about this. Arnold is one husband Edward does not want to hear about.

When the day at the office is over, I hurry to the station. There are two trains. If I run, I can make the first one. If I don't run, I have to wait twenty-five minutes. My car is parked in the lot at the other end. From station to home takes four minutes. Arnold could get four hard-ons in half the time.

Most of the people who work for my firm have been divorced at least once. They celebrate each new divorce. We're the norm, they say. It is possible that I may be the person divorced the most. I believe that in discussions not including me it has been decided that I was always the one at fault. No one comes right out and says that. It's how I interpret the silences.

When I was married to Potter, I was once unfaithful. The man was Eleazar Wells. Eleazar came up to me at a party, kissed the back of my neck, and whispered that I was the woman with whom he would most like to sleep. Possess! he said. Have! Sleep with! Strip bare, take naked! Eleazar was married at the time.

He tormented me. His conversations became more explicit every time we met. His fantasies were well-documented. The things he said we would do I'd seen verified in books.

In March, Eleazar divorced Gertie Vodel. We decided to meet the day the papers were signed. A tryst! he said. An assignation! A symphony of the bodies! I took a subway and a crosstown bus to his apartment. I cleaned the place, Eleazar said. I cleaned the place for you. We went into the bedroom and took off our clothes. Just being unfaithful might have been exciting. But Eleazar had built up my hopes too much. I, for one, don't think Gertie Vodel was the guilty party.

The people in my office are amused that I live in the suburbs. It sounds funny to them. Not for a single woman, they say. It separates me, I know. I cannot be called at a moment's notice to go anywhere. You miss everything, they say. What do you do? I go home, I say. I listen to the news as I prepare the meal. I live a life of deep contemplation.

Stephen left me in the early spring. I'm sorry, he said. He spoke of a woman. He said that her silken, uncorseted body had seduced him. It was impossible to resist. He said that he met her on a train. Another time he said that he met her in a restaurant. Actually, he met her in the apartment. She sat on our couch, stirred her drink in our glass, enticed him. Her name was Vina.

One evening I run along the streets hoping to catch the first train. I see a man and a girl in front of me. I slow down and do not pass them. I am certain it's Abby and her father. They are the right height and right shape. These are familiar backs. But the mutated hair could be anyone's.

I make arrangements. At the end of the week, I have another job. I am going to go to work in the suburbs. Nothing like a change, my mother once said.

There is the possibility of a new lover, even a marriage. If I married again, no one in the city would approve. More than your share, they would say. It's different in the suburbs. In the suburbs, no one knows anything. In the city, everyone knows everything—and while I was here, I knew too.

THE
HOBBYIST

○　○　○　○　○　○　○　○　○

Mrs. B. killed her spastic child. She had been driven to the
limits of her endurance. We'll stick by her, the neighbors said.
She is a saint. Due to a temporary loss of spirit, I am empty.
As empty as the mysterious Mr. B., drained of those highly-
touted life-juices.

I feel much better now, thank you. It was quite a shock,
of course. Seeing the blood and all. Bludgeoned, just as the
papers said. Terrible thing. Poor Mrs. B. She was driven to the
limits of endurance.

Mrs. Settle wished that Mr. Settle's father would die. She
wished it for a long time, and finally Mr. Settle's father died.
Then Mrs. Settle looked at the faces of her children and won-
dered if they were waiting too. It was only natural, the turning
of the generations.

Take a deep breath, he said. I won't let you drown. She
said, Cross your heart and hope to die?

This is basically an account of how Mrs. Settle drowned,
the killing of Mrs. B.'s spastic child, or the patricide of someone named Cissie S.

First of all, let me tell you that I am all right. In the pink, despite all that has happened to me. Despite the fact that the people I know seem to be acting inexplicably. For instance, Cissie S. Her father lies on the kitchen floor, the knife in his back. The floor is strewn with glass. I say poor Cissie was driven to the limits of her endurance.

When I was a child, my parents often took me to those evenings of family entertainment at my father's lodge or at the Legion Hall. Sooner or later a man would stand up and touch two fingers to his forehead. "Is there a gentleman in the audience with the initials S.J.?" From there he would go on to tell us S.J.'s age and occupation. The man never picked a child. He never picked me. "Miss L.M., in your handbag, there is . . . let me see . . . it is coming . . . yes, it is a handkerchief. A handkerchief with a small embroidered flower. I believe that it is a rose. Yes, a blue rose." A collective sound as Miss L.M. wafts her handkerchief aloft. White handkerchief, small blue rose.

Your grandparents' apartment must be vacated by the thirtieth, my husband says. Either do it or don't.

Of course, I will do it. First, I assemble the materials: broom, mop, pail, sponges, plastic trash bags, large and small.

After my grandfather died, my grandmother went to California to live in Venice with her sister-in-law Aurelia. My grandmother is seventy-three but in good health and a sturdy woman. I have no heart for the debris of my life, she wrote to me. My clothes are packed and a few staples of existence to contribute to Aurelia's housekeeping. Here is the key to my apartment. Please close up, sell, destroy, or otherwise dispose of all that is there. Love, Grandmother.

Without sentiment, my mother says sadly when I read the letter to her. Nevertheless, my mother says, you must do it. She would not want me poking among her things. Not me, I can tell you.

Time for examining, cleaning, and vacating the apartment will be between ten in the morning and four in the afternoon. I do not want you in that neighborhood after dark, my husband says. Muggers, rapists, junkies everywhere.

○ ○
○

I will find little of value in my grandparents' apartment. My grandfather had been a follower of Plekhanov and Axelrod, and therefore not a follower of possessions.

I arrange for a truck to take the furniture to a Hadassah Thrift Shop. Much will be abandoned as garbage. Bills, pictures, letters, great heights of paper. I rip until my hands ache. It's this notion I have about things like these, that they must be torn at least in half should a wind try to blow them back to the scene of the crime. Picture of unknown elderly couple found clutched in hand of stabbed father of Cissie S. Bill for refrigerator on floor near battered body of spastic child.

Some of the letters I find are written in English. I read them. They are about Ossipovich, emancipation, Kazan, Kuibyshev, Krasnoarmeysk, Sirion, semantic arguments, scandal, will Jair marry Beulah, Sholono's divorce. Their complexity frightens me. My life will never be as deep as this.

My grandfather died at eighty-two. He was a tall, remote man who had not been happy in the last years. In the opinion of the family, he welcomed death. He had been buried according to his detailed instructions in a nonsectarian cemetery with neither ceremony nor eulogy. A follower of Plekhanov and Axelrod does not weaken in the end. When my grandmother dies, she will be buried in California in the Orthodox manner. She, after all, is as tough as he was. Forty-eight years of marriage.

My grandfather had very few clothes. My grandmother had never bothered to discard them. A black suit, brown pants, underwear, socks. I stuff them into a large plastic bag and then I throw the bag out.

I have been working in the apartment for a day and a half. I could have finished sooner. But my husband keeps insisting that I leave the building before dark. Remember, he says. Muggers, he says, rapists, and also junkies. So when I pass other occupants of this building, I stay close to the wall and move warily. They do likewise.

The next tenant waiting anxiously to claim the apartment, her money already paid under the table, has come to see me. All this I will leave you, I tell her. The bed and dresser, the stove, the refrigerator, the Formica-topped table with two matching chairs.

o o
o

Not a marriage made in heaven, relatives said. He was me-shugga, my grandmother declared. He shames the family with nonsense. What will people say?

This is how I see her. She is wiping her hands on a white apron. She is a short, stocky woman in the middle of something emotional. Worrying about the neighbors. Worrying about appearances. It's a good act. A little blue rose. She yearned to be a martyr. With her brother she had run a printing press. For the revolution, she said, and displayed her fist.

As for my grandfather, his hobby was collecting dust.

I find the collection in four specially constructed cartons beneath my grandfather's bed. Each carton has layers of cardboard, and each layer is sectioned like an egg crate except that the spaces are much smaller, and in each space there is a tiny bottle, and on it a tiny label.

I haul the cartons into the kitchen and call my mother. Yes, she says. It is true. Father always collected dust. A very idiosyncratic man. But it's perfect, I say. And he put the dust into labeled bottles. Did you know that? I guess I did, my mother says, but I'd forgotten. I haven't thought about it in years. My father was an odd one.

So my grandfather was an odd one. I take up a bottle. The writing is legible, the ink faded to brown. *Hallway. Our apartment 8A. April 12, 1917.* I hold the glass up to the light. Gray fuzzy dust. The dustmop variety.

There were bottles with addresses on the labels and dates that covered decades. Dust from everywhere. Dust marking events. *T.S. Rich & Company. July 13, 1924.* Why from there?

It would take days to go through them all. So I took the cartons home. They're all that I took.

The doorman at my building piles the boxes onto a dolly and takes them up the back way. In here, I say, and show him the spot in the hall closet. Home at last, my husband says. He does not ask me what is in the boxes. Esther, the daughter, doesn't ask, either. Wilson, the son, is also not interested. I study my children, their placid blue eyes. What has happened to youthful curiosity? "Yuk," my daughter says and steps away from my outstretched arms. "You're all dirty."

Where are the offices of T.S. Rich & Company in July, 1924? And what about the sidewalk at Eighth Street near the florist in 1927? Don't know, my grandmother writes back in tiny, grudging letters. Throw those boxes out. Disease, mold, germs. Think of your children.

My grandfather was twenty-two when he arrived in this country, a political exile. My grandmother arrived two years later, a political exile too. They were married when my grandfather was thirty-four. In 1929, he gathered a sample of dust from beneath the bed of G.C. I cannot write my grandmother and ask who G.C. was. In 1929, my grandparents were married. Those are not my grandmother's initials.

Dust from Halley's Comet. 1910. My grandfather's flights from sidewalks. And this one. *Meteoric matter. September 9, 1925.* Cousins Julius and Ilyïch got him his first job in a coat and suit factory. But he had no talent for thread. No glad-hand manner for selling. A careless and lazy peddler. What will we do with you? they said. He worked happily for a time as a janitor's assistant in an office building. It doesn't matter, he said. I like it.

After he married my grandmother, they used her savings to open a store selling yard goods and linens. Business? the family said. Those two? Give it a month. They were wrong. My grandmother learned about accounts and about remembering to lower the awning against the sun. She became street-shrewd. She became a tradeswoman.

The store on Essex Street. 1923. It is ash-white. Stores are everywhere on that block. One sells tallithim, phylacteries, prayer books, and other religious needs. My grandparents moved uptown sometime in the Twenties.

From rucksacks of three refugees. 1939. You still lived at home, I say to my mother. Who came to the house in 1939? Are you raving mad? my mother says. I went to school. I was a schoolgirl. My father said to me, Study. Certainly, there were people in the house. What did I care? Anyway, they're all dead now.

My grandfather came to my high-school graduation party. He was already an old man who walked with a cane, cataracts growing over both eyes. The following year he had an operation, and his sight was mostly restored. But that day he could barely see. Kiss your grandfather, I was told, and I kissed the cheek that was offered so indifferently.

From walk with three people prior to departure. August 2, 1930. Among the things I do at this time are plan dinners, go to the theater, face my fears firmly. Could I do less? Once I said to my husband that I would rather be dead than one of those old women hoping to make the other side of the street before the light changes. He said, All things come to that.

From store on 93rd Street. Blood on this dust. 1935. The store was robbed, my mother says. They started to hit your grandmother, and my father became furious. He was a big man. He went after the two men and in the fight he stabbed one of them with the man's own knife. He was a hero on the street for days, but it made him sick. He couldn't eat. Violence was against his principles.

Dust from volcanic activity. In New York? Had he ever left the city? No, everyone says. His wife and children went to the country during the summer one year when money was easier. But he never went anywhere. He stayed home. No one remembers him leaving for anywhere. But perhaps they weren't paying attention.

Write me no more questions, my grandmother insists. Enough. Must this dust pursue me to my grave?

My husband and I are having an argument. It has lasted

for three days. We are going through the silent phase. Only when absolutely necessary will we speak to each other. At night, with the aid of a flashlight, I turn inside-out the empty pockets of his clothing. Nothing can be scraped from the pockets of his trousers. From the pockets of his jacket there is not one jot of fuzz.

Twice in his life, my grandfather's sight failed. Both periods lasted more than a year. The glass bottles dwindled during those times. Those that were filled were labeled with some code of X's large and small. He never relabeled those bottles. I can't break the code.

In the late Thirties, he must have taken a mistress. *Dust from dress of R. Dust by bed of R. Dust near door of R.'s room. 1938.*

R. has gone. I have fumbled quickly through the next few years of bottles. R. does not reappear.

Great Dust Storm of 1933. Sent to me by friend. Motes, specks, microns, millimicrons.

In the Forties there is dust from the grave of Joel. He is the son-in-law who died in the war. He was the father of my cousin Max, whose mother has married again and lives in Phoenix. He was a brilliant boy, Joel. Everyone says that.

Most of the dust has faded to white or pale gray. It has the consistency of powdery ash. Some, however, still has color. These are some of the colors. Brown, both light and dark. Coffee-brown, khaki, olive-brown, copper. Deep black and soot-black. Pearl-white. Sober-gray, gray-black, iron-gray.

One day my husband calls me into the small room used as his office at home. Have you a moment? he says. Certainly, I say, and follow him into the room. He closes the door. You have been very preoccupied, he says. You are always shut away somewhere, he says. You are mistaken, I say. I am here as always. I am home. You've been in a daze, he says. Did you think the children wouldn't notice? I had no idea, I say. They wanted to know what you were doing, he says. They spied on me? I say. Not at all, he says. They merely wanted to know what their mother was doing shut away so much by herself. They saw you pulling those cartons from the closet into the bedroom. It was only natural that they should look inside. I looked too, he says. And although I am tolerant, I want that dust out of this house. I'm warning you.

As it happens, I say, I was planning to do just that. I have finished my examination of the bottles.

Well then, he says. That's fine.

The dust is gone. My grandmother lives in Venice in an area of old women. She totters across the street hoping to escape the changing light and the energies of the cars. Mrs. B. walks the neighborhood scot-free. Cissie S. does her sleeping in an asylum. The circumstances of Mrs. Settle's death are declared an accident. The mind reader is still guessing ages and occupations.

Sometimes, for comfort, I whisper to myself the great dust words of the world.

Khamsin, Gibleh, Haboob.

○ ○ ○ ○

FROM P
FORWARD

The first graph that I created was a present for Chris and Ginger. I gave it to them on their tenth wedding anniversary. It was called the *Graph of Happiness*. The abscissa was divided into the years of their marriage. The ordinate on an arbitrary scale of 1 to 10 gave the emotional climate. I knew Chris and Ginger quite well, so the graph bore that touch of authenticity that was later to make my work so popular. There was the dip during the fourth year of their marriage when Ginger began to gain weight. There was the crescendo until the eighth year when Chris had that trouble with a cocktail waitress. Other slight waverings were duly recorded and indicated in the legend.

I remember my pleasure in devising that first graph. I printed it on white cardboard with a Montblanc filled with India ink, inserting the finished work in a ready-made diploma frame. Soon after, I was asked to do a graph for a child's birthday. I made a bar graph on dark blue paper, gold ink to represent the nine years of Melissa by height and weight. Her mother was naturally thrilled.

That was my early work. But I am not belittling it. I have great respect for the simplicity of my first attempts. One took a fact and translated it into a given point *(P)*. Anything was possible from *P* forward—the strophoid, the semicubical parabola, the Bowditch curve, the spiral of Archimedes.

o o
o

It is a period of slight desperation in our marriage, and so Milton is going away. Milton is going to Chicago. I am congratulated by friends who interpret this as a divorce or legal separation. I say no, it is neither. Milton is going to Chicago in order to find work.

Hard upon the decline in our fortunes, Milton and I sat down across from each other to discuss reality at the kitchen table. Belt-tightening time, Milton says, and reaches under the table to pinch my thigh.

He will try the job in Chicago. It does not pay for us to pull up stakes, the job in Chicago being very chancy. At any rate, my fees for graphs will sustain the apartment for a while. I will therefore stay behind with the child. Milton will take the Buick and head west. We have a night of impassioned farewells.

In truth, I am left behind with the child. The child takes the change very well. She knows about money. Fear not, Milton told her, a temporary relocation.

o o
o

The child's school is gray stone and takes up one square block. All the windows on the first floor are grilled against vandalism. I have walked around the building. In sixth grade, the girls are twelve. It is a difficult time.

"I met the mother of a friend of yours outside school today."

The child chews on a pencil as she does her homework. She nods.

"Who?"

"Someone named Cele."

The child looks at me cautiously. "I like her," she says. "We sit across the aisle."

"What kind of girl is she?"

"Weird," the child murmurs. "Lots of fun. She was kicked out of three schools. She says that in one school she was examined for witchcraft. Only I don't believe it."

I shudder. "Why witchcraft?"

"Cele has visions. They don't happen at school, though. But she talks about them. Says they mean love the Lord."

"She must be very peculiar," I say.

"No," the child says sharply. "She just sounds that way. You don't even know her. Besides, you can't stay in school all day and not talk to somebody."

○ ○
○

Cele is invited for a Saturday afternoon. She arrives in time for lunch, which, at the child's request, will be tunafish sandwiches, Cele's favorite. Later, the girls will go to the movies.

The child introduces her friend to me. This is Cele M. There are fourteen letters in her last name, so Mrs. Parker calls her Cele M. If the teacher were to continue mispronouncing her name, Cele would have her feelings hurt.

"Sounds perfectly sensible," I say.

○ ○
○

Mrs. M. and I meet by accident the next week and have coffee. "As a matter of fact," Mrs. M. says, "I think that my Cele said that she and your girl were best friends, and it pleases me no end. Things have been hard for Cele. This is her fourth school in three years. Confidentially," and Mrs. M. leans closer, "Cele has visions."

"Good grief," I say. "Visions of what?"

Mrs. M. whispers. "Cele won't say."

○ ○
○

I have a great deal of time to devote to the development of my graphs. Milton writes and tells me not to overdo. We are not poor. It is a setback. Milton has great confidence in himself. Still, I have dismissed the cleaning woman, the butcher, the greengrocer, the exercise class. I understand the psychology of this setback. It is logical that I feel unworthy and patched.

I make a nomograph for the Musser divorce. A detailed analysis of time-together allotments. Let X stand for Mr. Musser. I have begun to study Cartesian geometry. Musser is intensely pleased with the delicacy of his graph. I have done it on bristol board with a fine-nibbed pen. The result is an ellipsis.

I write and tell Milton everything. He sends me back the following messages:

1. You just want something to happen, and something will.

2. Cele is a bad influence. Under normal circumstances, you'd see that.

3. They are nuts. What is the matter with you?

○ ○
○

When I am sitting at my desk with the good reading lamp shining and a graph to be done, I am deeply happy.

The variations between curves are greater than I ever imagined. Business curves are wave curves without external significance. However, years of marriage, divorce, depression, and achievement yield significant similarities among people. S.R. has a relationship/hate curve with peaks to mark affairs. These receive random identifying letters explained in the captions below. S.R. loved the chart and wanted it framed. I now have a working arrangement with a framer. As a good customer, I get a referral fee. I realize that basically I wish to create more than two-dimensional curves.

I am doing a series of miniatures based on Milton's letters. They depict job progress, level of depression, length of time in Chicago. They are beautiful, these miniature charts, like Persian drawings.

○ ○
○

Mrs. M. telephones. "No way they can touch her. I know this from Legal Aid. She is not a disruption. Good student. Not tardy, not delinquent. Can't touch her. Not in fifty million years."

Milton sends me a wonderful letter. My dearest, he writes. All is cold and lonely here. I am determined to succeed for you. Keep me in your thoughts. Take care of the kid.

The summer the child went to camp at Lake Saranac, Milton and I weren't speaking. When we went upstate to visit her, we stayed in a little motel, the kind with neon signs that blink and blink. I wore aqua pajamas trimmed with deep green satin and with frog closings. That night in bed, Milton reached for me and opened my top. I felt his hand touch my breast.

"Get off me," I said and turned from him to face the wall.

○ ○
○

I am told that Cele fell into a trance at school. Here is what may have happened afterward.

EXAMINER: What do you see?

CELE: Not persons exactly. Sometimes it is just a feeling of someone. Sometimes lots of people. Sometimes just a lady.

EXAMINER: Why you?

CELE: Purity of spirit.

EXAMINER: My dear child, you are a mere snip of a thing, neither overly bright nor impressive. Furthermore, there is a record of truancy, shoplifting, unruliness.

CELE: Nevertheless, I see.

EXAMINER: What do these visions mean?

CELE: Don't know yet.

I see Musser occasionally. We've become lovers. He is a kind, even a gentle, lover. But in bed he weeps. He holds me close and whispers his wife's name.

Milton never did that.

Mrs. Parker sits me down opposite her desk. She pulls out a box of milk chocolates. "Here," she whispers, "have one."

"Your child is a very bright child," Mrs. Parker begins. "But we must recognize that she is susceptible. I mean, she isn't the usual child we get here. She isn't typical."

"The child is a child," I say.

"Oh no," Mrs. Parker says. "She has read so widely. It's her social development that I want to discuss. She is spending a great deal of time with Cele M."

"She is," I say.

"We are investigating," Mrs. Parker says. "I don't want you to think that the school system is without interest. Cele M. may have a problem."

"She has visions," I say.

"Ah." Mrs. Parker breathes a sigh and opens her eyes wider. "If you could encourage your child to seek other companions, I think that would be for the best."

"Everything's for the best," I say.

o o
o

Evenings, I stare across the room at the child sprawled on the floor doing her homework. She looks guileless and readable, but that is false. She has slipped onward. I can no longer encompass her experiences. Tell me how you feel? Tell me what it means? Sometimes, I find it hard to believe in her existence.

I do a depth curve of my feeling for the child. I do it in washes of magenta, green, and yellow. Curiously, it is not garish, but soft and flowing. I do not caption nor identify points.

I look up saints and shrines in the public library. I read about the Maid of Orleans, Hildegarde, St. Catherine of Siena, St. Genevieve, Abraham, Moses, Joshua.

"Promise me you won't tell anyone," the child says as I brush her hair. She is warm and flushed from her bath. She sits sipping her cup of hot chocolate.

"I promise," I say.

"Cele cured someone," the child says.

"Come now," I said lightly. "Surely you don't believe that."

"A beggar," my daughter persists. "A lame beggar on Seventh Avenue. Cele said that she didn't know it was going to happen. She just went over and touched his leg under a whole pile of dirty rags. Ecch. He rose right up."

"Terrific," I say, and go on brushing. "Who witnessed this curing?"

"No one," the child says. "Cele was alone. She was so frightened, she ran away."

I try to get a look at the child's face. But the long hair floats over it and obscures the eyes.

Milton sends a love letter. My dearest, I miss you terribly and wait anxiously to return to you. Take care of the child.

I devote myself to my work. I take another lover. Milton

comes home in the spring. "Money-wise," he says, "we have more than we had before." We embrace.

Everything changes. I have a well-received showing of my graphs. The child is doing tip-top in school. Milton is involved in speculations.

○ ○
○

One day I see Cele. She has grown much taller and is very thin. The shape of her bones is a pleasure to see.

"Mrs. R., hello, how are you?"

"Fine, Cele. How are things?"

"We're going to California. The end of the month."

"Well," I say, "give your mother my best."

"Will do," she says and runs off.

"The visions?" I call out. "What about the visions?"

Cele didn't hear. Or she did. The truth is, I don't know. She sees things. But that scarcely means she hears them. At any rate, it gives me an idea for a new graph, something to be titled *Reverses*. It will take vast sheets of paper, great costs in material. But who would put up the money for such a work? Except Milton, my speculator.

STORIES
UP TO A
POINT

I no longer go to the city very often. Still, every six weeks I turn up in the purple and white room where my hair is cut. Nona, who regularly does the work, is young and pretty. She is quite skilled. Being cared for this way is usually a pleasant experience. But today I have been kept waiting.

Nona detects my irritation, fusses unnecessarily with her brushes, and will not apologize. My hair has been washed by her assistant, Miriam, a girl of about the same age. Nona and Miriam seldom speak to each other unless it is about the details of their task.

Nona begins to comb out my hair. "It has been a hard week," she says. "You should have been here Wednesday. New customer. Woman around thirty. Elegant even in our smock. She no sooner sits down when orders spout. Your name? she asks poor Miriam. From that moment on, it's fetch me a tissue, Miriam. This coffee is too light and not hot enough, Miriam. Be a dear and run across the street and pick up my prescription, Miriam.

"See my counter?" Nona waves at it. The counter is bare

except for a bottle of blue disinfectant and a hand mirror.

"You know what the woman did?" Nona says. "She brought a lunch in a brown paper bag right from the deli. I tell you the smell of that pickle was terrible. She spreads her lunch on the counter. She unzips the briefcase on her lap and proceeds to write and eat. Her head is not still. Each clip of the scissors takes five minutes. I am beside myself. Madame, I begin. But she pays no attention. Finally, there is an apple. Do you have any idea of what an apple does?" I shake my head. "An apple makes the head bob." Nona demonstrates. "So she bites into that apple just as the blades of my scissors are closing. The scissors moved. The line was broken. She sensed it. It was in the back, and she couldn't see, but she sensed it. Ruined, she shrieks. You've ruined me! It was only a little V-shape cut. Real little. It could be fixed. A slight alteration of the style. The woman is screaming and she's grabbing the mirror to look. Caused a scene. We took her down the hall into a private booth used for coloring. I fixed the cut. Actually, it was an improvement. Shorter, more buoyant. I could see in her eyes that she thought so too. But, of course, hers was not the nature to admit this. Never before, she said. Never has this happened to me. So I told her it was on the house. No, she said. I will pay the usual rate. Poor Miriam has to clean up what's left of the lunch."

Nona is staring at me triumphantly.

○ ○
○

My husband burned everything in our daughter's room. He carried great armloads of books down the stairs. He made a bonfire of that room. On top of the pile of books he threw clothes still on hangers. Good woolen dresses, jumpers, blouses, three still with tags. He staggered under the weight of her records. She had a collection of 78's.

"Help me," he ordered. But I just leaned against the wall and watched. I had never seen his face that vicious before. He opened the windows of her room and flung to the yard the contents of her desk drawers.

"See?" my husband yelled. "See?"

The gasoline he siphoned from his Lincoln. He poured it over clothes, books, records. He lit a match and jumped back.

I watched from inside the kitchen. A few minutes later I heard the siren that summons the voluntary firemen. A neighbor had reported us. By the time the engine arrived, the flames had burned everything up. The grass on that part of the lawn was charred brown.

The firemen gave my husband a citation. They were very friendly about it. I served cold beer through the kitchen window. Later, my husband drove to the garden shop and bought squares of sod. He raked up the yard and put down the new grass.

○ ○
○

We do not discuss my husband's first wife. Their divorce took place before we met, so I bear no responsibility. Still, I wonder about her, and presume this is how the marriage ended.

"I am unhappy," Marlene says. "Everything feels so bitter, so useless." My husband makes verbal lists. "You are unhappy," he says, "because there is insufficient heat in the apartment, you spoke to my mother, and the Rosens are moving to a nicer place on Eighty-second." "That is not so,"

Marlene says. "You always want to make everything specific. You have no moods, only reasons." "My God, Marlene, misery is specific." Marlene chews on a hangnail. "Then if you are right, I am miserable about those things, and you cannot make me forget them. You ought to be able to do that." "I don't make you happy?" he says. "Didn't you just prove it?" Marlene says.

My husband sits down at the breakfast table and slams the *Times* across the toaster. "If she ever calls," he declares, "if she ever calls, you are to hang up at once, do you hear?" "I will," I reply. "No, wait," he says. "Don't do that. Talk to her first. But coldly. Let her ask to come home or for money. Then tell her about her room. Tell her how I sold everything—her furniture, her pictures. Be sure and tell her how I burned her papers, her books, her clothes, and her record collection. Tell her that her room is now an upstairs den. Mention the console television in the corner. She'll hate that." "I'll do just that," I say. "Swear it to me." "I swear," I say. "How do you want your toast?"

During the Thirties my aunt would hang down from a window to tap electricity to run a hot plate. My uncle would hold her by the legs to keep her from falling out. Theirs was the torment of people who kept losing money until they reached total poverty. Now my aunt has a three-carat diamond and a bracelet with sapphires.

○ ○
○

My husband and I were in a restaurant in the Village. Our table was near the door. A heavy blonde woman with a small boy came from somewhere in the back. I nudged my husband. "Look," I whispered. "It's Francesca." We stared at our plates and began to eat with earnest devotion so that glances would not meet and acknowledgments thus be necessary. Francesca went up to the counter with her bill.

"I'm sorry," she said exhibiting her black purse, "but I seem to have left home without my wallet. This is terribly embarrassing. I will come back with the money in the morning." "Have you any identification?" the man behind the counter asked. "If I had any identification," Francesca said with asperity, "then I would have my wallet."

"Let's go home, Mommy," said the child, whose name I did not know.

"All right," the man said. "Just sign your name and address on the back of the check."

Francesca wrote something and then read it aloud. "Alberta Sweet," she said.

○ ○
○

Sometimes I suffer from aboulia and sometimes from agrypnia. I am ill at ease with aunts. Yesterday, I misinterpreted a telephone message and ran screaming from the beauty parlor. People turned to look at me. I was very ashamed. How shall I face them again? But it might have been something terrible. Something terrible could have happened.

OFFSPRING
OF THE FIRST
○ GENERATION ○

One day it came to me that I was neither adopted nor the illegitimate daughter of the King of Rumania and Magda Lupescu. Everything, of course, has run downhill since then.

I have noticed that many people do not like me. As a result of analysis, a flood of repressed memories has run ashore. My analyst did not like me. I made an early decision to have two or three children, certain that when they grew up they would be of my blood and therefore would desire my company. I was wrong.

Lachman, my lover, pushes past the beaded curtain and walks into the kitchen. He is portly and dignified even in pajamas. In profile, he resembles the Swiss bankers and French magistrates whose grainy pictures are sometimes seen in newspapers.

"Why in hell don't you take these beads down? They grab at you like a centipede," he says.

"I mean to," I say. I am deferential. The beads are the last reminder of my daughter.

"How pale you are," Lachman says. He touches my

forehead. "Do you work too hard at the store?"

"Work at a store? Don't you know anything about me?"

"Well," he says and sits down. "You used to work at a store."

Lachman will be leaving me soon. He will have the choice of many women. Already weeks go by between his visits.

"It's been a long time," Lachman says. "What's the news?"

I clear my throat. "Harriet's husband left her. There are five children in the house. It is an unthinkable thing. There is an Eldorado in the driveway. The house is heavy with furniture. Willa Hoomes comes three times a week to clean the house. Morty Goldfarb's wife left him. They had three boys. Morty Jr., Titus, and Pender. Morty is a good man. He hopes one day to live on a farm."

"I've been thinking," Lachman says, "of trying California."

"Yes," I reply. I got over it before he even said it.

○ ○
○

I have aunts, uncles, many cousins. Their houses are filled with inheritances of hallmarked silver, translucent china, Kerman carpets. These abundant *landsleit* have gatherings, parties. I am seldom asked to join them. But I go, anyway.

I call someone and say, "See you on Sunday."

"At Duvey's?"

"Yes," I say. "At Duvey's." This is how I discover where they gather to eat themselves silly.

Also useful is a large calendar to mark anniversaries, birthdays. This way I can also project weddings and graduations.

Thus, I went to the wedding of Lueta and Talsman, ignoring the fact that their invitation to me went astray. I had to check with the three catering halls acceptable to the family in order to determine time and place.

I am not cheap. I send good gifts. For Lueta, I purchased a gold wine cup for ceremonial occasions. Gold objects are always twenty-four carat. The china I supply is neither cut-rate nor seconds. If the gift is cash, I think only in three figures.

I stand reasonably in the middle range of fashion. I cannot be pointed out in family pictures as strange. I appear in many photographs, slipping quickly into the last row before the shutter is snapped. In my family album, I have just pasted the latest picture. Lueta is a lovely bride in an old-fashioned wedding dress that belonged to her great-aunt. In my blue taffeta dress, I am third from the left in the row behind the bride's family.

My conduct is always decorous. No one will be embarrassed. I inquire about the state of your health and your family's. I remember to avoid the divorces, the other women, the wayward children, the failing of once-thriving businesses.

Yet I remain the one pushed from the pack. Alert to the instinctive lack of sympathy to be found in my species, I keep my grievances and despair to myself. My husband, who fell in front of a D train, died just before the divorce papers were filed. The funeral was a disgrace. The young woman at the graveside, who I observed was my cousin Sylvie, was in truth the woman my husband had planned to run off with.

Martin, my son of the five-hundred-dollar suits, has sources of money to tear out my heart. Leslie, who has married twice, lives somewhere in the West. Her mail is unforwardable.

Noam, my youngest son, is twenty-four and lives with me. We survive on the proceeds of my late husband's insurance wisely invested in utilities. Also, I have an income as a political pamphleteer. I can turn out the text of a pamphlet in four to eight hours. "Your Philosophy Is Mine" is my motto.

Noam was married to Abigail. She locked him out of their apartment after shouting abuse at him. She charged him with impotence, sodomy, lechery, and other vile behavior. He took his two suitcases and came home. "Leave me alone, Ma," he said, and walked down the hall to the spare bedroom.

I have known hard times, unpleasantness, fear. All of this I am unable to share. I do not for a moment accept isolation as the legitimate leitmotif of my life. Against the early signs of my shunning, I daily checked myself in the mirror. How do they know that I am not to be liked? Chosen last? I worked hard to be smart and pretty. I washed dishes for my mother, ran errands for my father, gave up the biggest piece for everybody.

One day Noam leaves his bedroom. "What is it?" he shouts. "I care. I am not unkind. They hate me for the right answer. They applaud my errors."

"Your blood is too good for transfusions," I say.

I want to help Noam. I have always been a follower of honorable causes. I worked in favor of peace. I am a registered voter. I contribute to the support of an Asian child.

Theories change. So I am investigating the possibility of analysis for Noam. The cost is robbery. The time deducted from life enormous. Noam will have forgotten his youth. And I know that if the smell of the litter is not on you, it is hopeless. Is there no cure for being disliked?

My parents did not enjoy my presence. On my wedding day, they whispered in the corner that I was pregnant, that the marriage was forced. During the ceremony, they stood like stones.

Young, pale Jonathan swayed beneath the canopy. Within a year, he was unfaithful—in less time than that, loathsome. His body could have fouled mine with disease.

Noam says, "Abigail grew to despise me. I was a good husband, generous, kind, ardent. You are nothing, she said to me. Never in a thousand years should I have married you."

I have shelves, drawers, boxes full of outlines and lists. They are useful in my work. One list is headed "Desirable Traits." I made this list when I was a schoolgirl. On the left side of the paper are the names of ten of the most popular girls I knew. Opposite each name are the qualities of personality that I surmised inspired admiration. Which traits didn't I possess? I had them all. Moreover, I was idealistic, honest, truthful. I observed that other children cheated at games, were lazy, practiced masturbation, lied.

How did I fail Noam? Was it something I didn't do when he was a child? But he never gave me any trouble. Whereas Martin was delinquent, truant, a scholastic failure. Leslie traded on her prettiness. I read to Noam. I cooked his meals, mended his clothes. Was it a button I maybe missed?

The note I slip under Noam's door says, "Return to work. Don't give up the ship."

Noam writes me a reply.

"I was a member of the management team. Responsibility was delegated to me, and I complied. I did not have my own secretary. I dictated onto an IBM belt in my portable hand-held unit. This belt then went to the typing pool. The work came back to me in large brown inter-office envelopes. Often, two or three days went by when no one spoke to me. At first, I was not concerned. The work was enough to fill the time. After a month or so, I noticed that I ate lunch alone. I tried all the nearby coffee shops. I saw only strangers. If I joined a group, they did not make me welcome. Their conversations dealt with matters I did not understand, and they would not explain."

○ ○
○

At parties, I join a group and cannot be removed. I have this skill for appropriate comments, witticisms, anecdotes. When someone gives a party, I volunteer to help the hostess. "Let me," I say, and reach for a bowl. I will serve, wash up, run to the store for whatever you forgot. When the party's over, I'm the first to say, "I'll drive you home. No need to call for a taxi."

Once I gave Ethel Lee twenty-five dollars in exchange for an invitation to her sixteenth birthday party. Was this the gift? It was not. The gift was a sterling silver, heart-shaped pin.

The city fills with dirty rain. There are filthy puddles every-where. My head aches with the falling barometer. Two leaves have dropped from my geranium plant. My body is swollen and poisoned.

My work schedule lags, I am so busy thinking about Noam. How can I help him? Although we do not speak when we pass in the hallway, I know it is from me that he expects deliver-ance. If I can help him, then he will love me forever, and forever we will celebrate holidays together.

I have heard that the old man upstairs has committed suicide. He used barbiturates to do it. He was a cartographer. We had been neighbors for years. But we never spoke. Sometimes, I would remark about the state of the weather. But the cartographer did not reply. His son and daughter-in-law came from Queens and carried his body away. If I die, there is a card I keep in my wallet. I have willed my organs. My underwear is clean.

Noam does not join me in the living room in the evenings. But his presence in the apartment is felt. I believe he weeps. The door to his room is locked. "Let me in," I beg.

Noam says one day, "I can't take it any more. I once had friends. People sometimes sought me out. I had Abigail. Mother!"

"Join a club," I tell him. "Write letters. Keep active."

I recopy the list of Desirable Traits into a single column minus the names of the girls. I push the list under Noam's door. "I cannot afford to support you!" I call through the door.

Noam takes a job.

"Try to be friendly," I tell him. "Dress neatly. Be confident. Check yourself in the mirror."

I drain my experiences. I try to find examples for Noam. Between the ages of eleven and seventeen, only three persons voluntarily spoke to me. Still, I moved in the world. I avoided eccentricities of behavior. My grades were good. I have had terrible quarrels. Martin and Leslie have yelled at me, denying our ties of blood. My late husband often threatened me. "I shall reveal you to the world," he would say. "Hateful! Despicable!" People have shouted at me. I have been the target of unjust accusations. But look at me now, a guest.

It's only a question of vision.

○ ○
○

Noam has begun to perk up. I leave his dinner warming in the oven while I retreat to my room. I have many assignments. The work goes well.

"I am being transferred to another city," Noam says. "It will be good for me." I agree, kiss his cheek, help him pack. I give him a check. The sum astonishes him. Also me.

"Send a letter," I implore. "Keep in touch."

He leaves me standing on the doorstep.

Noam writes that he has married. We did not have a real wedding, he says. Just a simple little ceremony.

Yet in my heart I know that her parents were there, weeping and toasting the blissful couple. I would have seen for myself if someone had invited me.

SCRATCH

I have a garden of memories I visit as needed. I've been thinking of pruning them. One last run-through and then out with the ones I don't need. I cannot begin my new life without some shedding. I plan to become a recluse.

Memory can be prodded with questions. For example, did the grass *bend* when the wind blew? Get the picture? Were there *blue* flowers on the dress? *Three* cousins playing tag on the beach?

Are these the right questions for a city girl? *How* dirty were the curtains? *What* scratched when you moved?

I used to say that I wanted a place in the country with a high barbed-wire fence. Randolph, my first husband, thought I was joking. Armel, my fifth husband, knew I was serious.

Never do, he said. All you'll get is more attention. To be solitary requires careful thought. Bear that in mind. Unusual dress, mannerisms, old shopping bags, white socks. Avoid them all.

I'll remember that.

At any rate, I have decided to withdraw. I have certain

fears, but they are not abnormal fears. Even my despair remains within proper limits. But I have no further desire for the society of people.

I've done a bit of research. I don't want to start off being funny. It is possible that in time I may appear ludicrous, but being funny I could not bear.

I have started by consulting real estate agents in the various boroughs. The choice of location will be made by house rather than by the reverse. Armel was right. A country road is quite out of the question. Rural vagrants. Jalopies full of boys with beer bottles. I'd be easy prey. No, I want an ordinary street convenient to transportation and with nearby stores.

The plan has been pushed back and forth in my thoughts. There was no unseemly revelation. No Eureka. But the symptoms of withdrawal have been with me for a long time. The desire not to list myself in important lists. The failure to put the right number on the line. I have been called to task. Mrs. Ruffino, after consulting my personnel file, has suggested that I see a gynecologist. Time of life, she says. Do you sweat? I don't know, I reply. I wonder if there are dark shadings under my arms. I've seen this before, Mrs. Ruffino insists.

○ ○
○

Did the father say, "You are going to spend the *summer* with your mother's family?" Was the girl *more* than willing? Did she, in fact, *beg* to go?

When the aunts met her at the railroad station, they remarked that she was pale. They thought it strange that in July she should still be pale. They held barbecues every Sunday in the back yard of the eldest aunt. For tables, they set up three sets of sawhorses and covered them with wooden planks. They made eight pounds of potato salad, twenty pounds of spareribs. Ten chickens glistened beneath a red coat of sauce.

The eldest aunt watched her often and did not fail to notice that she always chose to sit cross-legged on the grass.

"It's a beautiful table," the girl said.

She sold shoes in the basement of Shinder's. It was only a summer job, but she said that her hands always smelled of feet. Actually, she didn't help people try on shoes. All she did was stand in the opening in the middle of a square counter on which shoes tied together with bits of plastic were tumbled. People took the shoes themselves and tried them on. Sometimes they ripped apart the plastic ties. Sometimes they tried to combine a 7B with a 7A. It was her job to catch that. Check sizes before wrapping. Two of a kind, not two of different kinds. Sometimes they asked her to find sizes. She wasn't willing to help.

Her parents were business people. She was raised in an apartment with a concrete stoop in the front and garbage cans and clotheslines in the back. She believed, therefore, that grass bestowed tranquility and the true spirit of family life. She was twenty-three before she watered a lawn. The spiraling green rubber and the spray of water entranced her. She had three daughters, Winara, Lucille, and Lenore. Lenore was born with cerebral palsy, but the affliction was slight. Still, the child was tainted. To avoid looking at the girl, they sent her away to school at ten. She flourished there and was never really seen again.

o o
o

A brick house, I tell the real estate agents. I will not collect old newspapers, roll balls of foil, or hoard the droppings of cats. Who will be able to tell what road I have chosen? I shall be neatly dressed, my paths swept, my grounds in order. Eccentricities, those already mine, I will discard. No more black cigars, for example. The front parlor for the unwelcome caller will be lobby-tidy. Perhaps I will affect a cough. A red-cheeked hack of streaming suppurations. Watch them pull back in dread. Clean, but sickly. Pot of maidenfern on the hall table.

There must be a front lawn surrounded by hedge. The prior presence of a hedge is important. I will increase the height and the thickness. It shall, of course, remain neat. Clipped topiary. I will nod politely to the neighbors on the left and on the right. Quick! Inside before she speaks to us and becomes an acquaintance. Kin too shall drop away.

○ ○
○

It is a mid-nineteenth-century rosewood parlor table with a marble top. She derived a sensual pleasure from running her fingers over the scallops, the lozenges. The eldest aunt watched her often. She did not fail to notice that the girl always sat cross-legged on the carpet near the table.

One day the eldest aunt reached down and stroked her hair. "When you grow up, it shall be yours. Do you think you can wait for that?"

Good schools, the agent says. Ask anyone, the district is the best. I smile. No children, I say. The agent looks embarrassed. She pulls the fox collar of her gray coat tighter and unlocks the door.

It is a brick house, front yard hedged with trimmed arbor-vitae, two spruce trees hiding the windows from view.

Cut them back, the agent says. Light galore.

I walk into the small hall. This is the right house. The rooms are not large and drift one into the other. Only I shall wander room to room.

Nice kitchen, the agent says.

House as investment, I say. Place for my old age. Won't live here for years yet.

The agent nods approval.

I am more interested in the mechanics of the house than the agent thinks. I want to know what can possibly go wrong.

○ ○
○

What do you do for a living? Cooper asks.

I write letters.

You what? I smile. I write letters, I say. I make up letters to sell to various businesses. Letters of regret. Letters announcing sales. Letters of supplication for charities of infinite mercy. Letters of threatening intent. I am an expert on letters of threat veering not a jot off the mark.

Cooper kisses my lips. Deliberately rubbing his lips from side to side across my mouth to smear my lipstick in a wild, unseemly pattern.

Read me a letter, he begs.

My dear Madam, I read. We are pleased to announce that you have been selected to try our correspondence course of modern ballroom dance lessons in the privacy of your own home without embarrassment and the inconvenience of long contracts. Our charts shall make of you an enchantress, a Ginger Rogers, an Isadora Duncan. Our illustrations can be duplicated by your feet. A set of long-life plastic records accompanies this course. This opportunity will soon be withdrawn. Send for our introductory lesson, and you will never again sway on the sidelines.

Cooper pulls me to my feet.

Dear Madam, he begins.

○ ○
○

That last summer she brought from New York a set of skeleton keys for the simple locks on some of the doors. One afternoon she opened the closet in the breakfast room. It only required a quick turn of the third key tried.

The closet was like a small room. There were wooden shelves with piles of china. Bowls, vases, sets of dinner plates. Many were banded with gold. She took a small bowl and wrapped it in a handkerchief. She hid it in the pocket of her slacks. She closed the door and locked it.

There were tiny yellow chrysanthemums painted delicately across the bottom of the bowl. The edge was lobed and had two fine lines of gold circling it.

There was no denying it. She had stolen something.

She put it on her dresser at home. She had a story all prepared. She bought it at a rummage sale.

She kept straight pins in the bowl. After she was married, she put the bowl on a wide white windowsill in the living room.

She sat on the edge of the bed holding a stocking in her hands. She disliked putting on her stockings. She disliked all garments. She dreamed of wearing nothing and yearned to go to some country where the women went unclothed.

Her mother pinned a cloche to her head. Her father wore his scratchy suit. It was a fool thing, they said, encouraging her to go. Money for two years. What good was that? Who'd take care afterwards? Not them. Did she know what a working-man made?

She was dancing alone in the living room, moving gracefully around couch and chairs, arms floating upward. She touched nothing. She thought that she was draped in a loose-fitting robe. She didn't hear her parents enter.

Stop that, her mother said.

Her father scratched the needle across the phonograph record.

She was dancing.

For God's sake, her father said.

Her mother pulled down the shades. They went into the kitchen. Their cheeks were red. They shivered.

I'll make tea, her mother said.

They sat in the kitchen.

Sometimes she cannot remember the names of relatives. She was sick through the winter. She was sixteen. In the spring, they sent her to the eldest aunt. Others thought that it was a shame. To saddle an old woman with a sick child, or vice versa. But she recovered and was careful not to be a bother.

The table went upstairs when the eldest aunt could no longer walk. They turned the large front bedroom into a sitting room. They took down the flowered wallpaper, painted the room white. The table held a tea service. Sometimes, the eldest aunt would wink at her and say, "I won't scratch the table."

First, the grandfather was a peddler. He sold china. He had

his name on a building. He had plaques on the walls. But first
he sold china. He had all the china you ever heard about.
Meissen, Sevres, Chelsea, Doulton, Limoges, Belleek, Wedg-
wood. The china that wasn't sold is locked in a closet. It is of
great value. It mustn't be touched.

The hall is papered in stripes. Washable, the agent says.
All the paper is washable here. Like new. I mean, you can see
that.

○ ○
○

Armel is having trouble with his current wife. I don't know
why I left you, he says. He caresses my back, his fingers
drawing figures over my skin. The callused tip of his finger is
an exciting roughness. Something scratchy. I cannot remember
Armel when he was my husband. We lived in one, two rooms.
One day we had a discussion.

Then we had a wedding. I wore a white dress of *peau de
soie.* My brother got drunk. He said, She walks, she talks, she's
almost human. He said that I looked like an accident in white.
My mother was crying. Armel is in the corner drunk. You
should never have married, his mother is telling him.

He left the two rooms in the middle of winter. I was
wearing a new dress. The dress had wide padded shoulders. My
lips were a deep burgundy. He left for no special reason.

I swoon from the silence in every room. I could live like
a monk, a celibate, a contemplative without the strictures. My
rooms, those beyond the public eye, will be simple. My bed has
a metal frame. The mattress has a guarantee for life. Buy
sturdy. No repairs. No breakage.

It was easy to unpack.

The bare rooms thrill me. I could dance in them. Through them. My toes smoothing the wood. Nothing scratchy anywhere.

It was with the first shadows of twilight that I heard the ringing of the bell.

There they were crowding the porch. "Surprise!" they shouted. They carried covered casseroles and boxes with silver bows. Filing past me, they filled the house. They put the food in the kitchen. They opened bottles of wine and blew rings of smoke. Someone had a phonograph. Armel was there.

Sweets, he said and took me in his arms, I just couldn't stay away.

They put out their cigarettes in the soil of the maidenfern. They put their wet glasses on the top of the table. The etchings in the marble will be permanent.

○

CARE
BY WOMEN

Mrs. Triton had three daughters in quick succession—Sylvia, Sidonie, and Sandra. That's it, Mr. Triton said. Obviously, there is to be no son. Mrs. Triton knew that gender was determined by the father. But she saw no reason to make her husband unhappy. Why make a man unhappy?

The girls were pretty, picture-book children. And on good days when they ran to greet him with hugs and call him Daddy, Horace Triton felt things could certainly have been worse. Vera Triton was pleased with his attitude. Our babies, she said. Before the twirling little girls appeared, Mrs. Triton had graduated from college, marked time in a job, and, fulfilling all expectations, married.

Mrs. Triton's friends said that a daughter was a daughter all the days of your life. Mrs. Triton agreed. On winter Saturdays rosy with cold, Mrs. Triton and the girls went to matinees and shopped at Lord & Taylor. Salesgirls admired the girls because they were well-behaved, patterning themselves after Sylvia, who was the oldest and docile by nature.

Sylvia at eighteen did not enter college as planned. Instead, she went to a Home for Unwed Mothers in Chicago near Mrs. Triton's sister, Ethel. Ethel made all the arrangements. Mrs. Triton wept for days. Mr. Triton kept his silence. He feared the possible destructiveness of his words. Sidonie said to her sister, You're dumb. Don't you know anything? Sandra, taking advantage of everyone's preoccupation, stayed out until midnight five nights in a row.

Sometimes Mrs. Triton thought that she would collapse from the ache in her heart. She had tried to make their lives perfect. Perhaps she should have been more careful. But they never wanted to listen. Skip to the exciting parts, Sidonie would say. Perhaps she should have told them about how Grandma got carted off to prison. For politics, Mrs. Triton would say. Only for politics. Never for being too free.

After the birth of the baby, Sylvia and child went to California. A child belongs with its natural mother, Sylvia said. That's what it's all about. Mrs. Triton sent money for Sylvia to enroll in college and also to pay for a sitter.

o o
o

Mrs. Triton from earliest memory was the daughter of a widow. My heart belongs to the people, Mrs. Triton's mother used to say. The call of the people took her away. Mrs. Triton's childhood was therefore passed in the care of others.

It was thinking about her mother that made Mrs. Triton decide to see Natalie. Natalie, a friend with whom Mrs. Triton had shared the fearful hours of youth, would understand. It was safe to confide in Natalie, since Natalie had nothing to do with anything.

"It will pass," Natalie said after hearing about Sylvia. "These children. They don't know what life is all about. I will make some tea."

The tears flowed abundantly from Mrs. Triton's eyes. She had been right to seek comfort from Natalie. Hadn't they been the best of school friends? Hadn't they the bond of their mothers' politics? Hadn't their mothers been written about in the newspapers and also gone twice to jail? Better still, there were no fathers.

Mrs. Triton dried her eyes and stared at Natalie. Natalie's hips had gotten heavy. Natalie had gotten to be a big, strong-looking woman married to a professor of anthropology.

"Life was easier," Mrs. Triton said, "when we were young. Life was all possibilities. Do you remember the Young League? So full of idealism. Times are different now. Times are very hard."

"Maybe," Natalie said. "Anyway, I never joined the League."

"Isn't that strange?" Mrs. Triton said. "How could I forget? I was so certain that you were there with me. At the meetings, I mean." She stood up.

"Stay for dinner. Izzie and the boys will be home soon."

"No," Mrs. Triton said. "I have my own family, thank you."

o o
o

Sidonie, who everyone said was bright as a button, went to college. Mrs. Triton noticed that at some time Sidonie had stopped being pretty. She had put on a lot of weight and her complexion had gone bad. Twice Sidonie had yelled at her mother that if Mrs. Triton didn't like it, she knew where she could go.

Mrs. Triton saw an analyst about her crying. The tears, she said, don't stop. You're not in a state of acute depression, the analyst said. Things are difficult everywhere. He also said, Live and let live.

The Tritons owned a handsome house surrounded by a large, well-tended garden. The house had been built in 1815. The doors still had their original hardware. However, the train ride to the city took an hour. Ten hours a week, Mr. Triton said to his wife. To and from. I know, Mrs. Triton replied. She always checked the liquor levels. Mr. Triton liked his Scotch as soon as he arrived home.

Sidonie shared a flat on Amsterdam Avenue with three girls and two boys. She was a Poli Sci major. She made Phi Beta Kappa in her junior year. She was going to become a lawyer and get *them*. One day she fell in love and quit school. She went to live in Oregon. But first she lost thirty-five pounds. She was now so dark-eyed and fragile that the filthy language she used was an even bigger shock.

Sandra did things so terrible, Sidonie threatened to call Sylvia. Then Sylvia called back and asked to speak to Sandra. Sandra was on the phone a long time. Sandra's end of the conversation was silence. Mrs. Triton kept Mr. Triton from listening in on the extension. There are some things, Mrs. Triton said, that a mother and father shouldn't hear.

It was decided to send Sandra to Sylvia since Sylvia took no crap. Mr. Triton put her on a plane. He stayed in the terminal and drank awhile. Bitches, he said out loud. People at the bar turned to stare. Bitches, Mr. Triton said, and lifted up his Scotch.

Mr. and Mrs. Triton were very careful with each other after all the girls were gone. They went to dinner, they went to concerts, they went to Europe. Mr. Triton began to pay attention to the changing times. Mrs. Triton began exhibiting her flowers at plant shows. Extroversion is the ticket, the analyst advised. Mingle. Mrs. Triton was impressed with the depth of that thinking.

She visited Natalie twice. Natalie was having trouble with her marriage. There had been someone a year ago. "But it was nothing," Natalie said. "Nothing. He broke it up, and I've tried to be understanding."

"I know," Mrs. Triton said. "We need to be more like our mothers. We need to be stronger."

"They weren't so strong," Natalie said.

Mr. Triton dropped out one afternoon four years after the last girl left. It couldn't have happened in one afternoon, but Mrs. Triton always described it that way. I had no idea, she later said. He just came home, packed two suitcases, said good-bye. It was in the afternoon.

Mr. Triton deeded her the house. Liquidated his business and divided the money. He guaranteed Mrs. Triton a reasonable income. Horace, Mrs. Triton had wept. This is madness. Is there another woman?

Mr. Triton shook his head. Not yet, he said. But I'm off to San Francisco. He patted Mrs. Triton's shoulder. If only we'd had a son, he said.

○ ○
○

Sometimes Sidonie's travels took her to the city. When they did, she called Mrs. Triton. Hello, Sidonie said. It's me. They met on a street corner. Sidonie kept her mother waiting. It wasn't deliberate, Sidonie said. Mrs. Triton selected a plain cloth coat to wear for these meetings. But she never succeeded in not looking well-dressed. Sidonie would stare at Mrs. Triton in contempt. Values, she'd say. Values. They'd shake hands, and Mrs. Triton felt the firm clasp of those rough, callused fingers. Sidonie was into a lesbian phase. They ate lunch at an Orange Julius. When the hour was up, Mrs. Triton put a folded twenty into Sidonie's hand. For your last birthday, Mrs. Triton said.

Mrs. Triton had a grandson in California whose name was Bird. She had never seen him. She continued to live in the house and go to plant shows. She met a widower in the local library one day, and let him take her home. In the morning, Mrs. Triton did not feel guilty. But neither did she feel particularly wonderful. So that is over, she told herself. She looked at her garden. Bird, she said out loud, is a stupid name for a child.

She went to see Natalie more often. Natalie kept talking about leaving Izzy. I want to, Natalie said. But what about the boys? To leave now would be selfish. Don't you think so?

Mrs. Triton nodded in agreement.

I'm trying to be sensible, Natalie said. I look at my watch before I go out. Ten o'clock. He's lecturing. Two o'clock. He's meeting with the Dean. It works. If I can just keep it up.

Mrs. Triton wrote a story about plants for her suburban newspaper. She called it "Plants Do the Funniest Things." The newspaper made it a regular feature. Mrs. Triton was pleased. She had an affair with a man named Arthur. He was twenty years her junior, a nice-looking man, twenty years her junior. But it didn't last a week. Our memories, she said. We remember different things.

She was writing a book about plants and family life when she had to arrange for a lawyer for Sandra. Mrs. Triton flew to the city where Sandra was in jail. She cried throughout the entire flight. Sandra told her to pay the lawyer and get lost.

Everything changed. Her house no longer suited her. Her garden was no longer a pleasure. The long train ride. Who needs it? she said, and sold what was in it at auction and put the house up for sale. It sold within the month. It's darling, the doctor's wife said, just perfect for us and the kids.

Mrs. Triton moved to the city. She furnished her new apartment. She made new friends. She took some courses at the university. She was anxious to discard the appearance of the suburban woman. Her number was unlisted.

Sylvia and Bird came to the city and could not find Mrs. Triton. The old lady has skipped, Sylvia told her son. Then Sylvia remembered Raven & Cross, her mother's lawyers. Mrs. Triton is traveling in Italy, Mr. Raven said. He offered Sylvia fifty dollars. He was certain that Mrs. Triton would approve.

Mrs. Triton was riding in a yellow sports car with a man named Walter. They were going to Connecticut for the weekend. Mrs. Triton knew the road. Would you mind, she asked Walter, if we went out of our way a little bit? I'd like to see a house I once owned.

The house looked the same. No sign of anyone around. Mrs. Triton decided to take the chance. She went around back to look at the garden. That's when she realized it was the wrong house.

Oh well, she said out loud.

"I remembered something the other evening," Mrs. Triton said to Natalie. "I remembered that you used to pick on me."

"Did I?" Natalie frowned.

"That's right," Mrs. Triton said. "When I wouldn't do what you wanted, you'd push me down and sit on my neck."

Natalie shrugged. "Not that often," Natalie said.

"Often," Mrs. Triton said. "It was often. I never realized this before. I thought we suffered equally."

"I don't know that it was really like that," Natalie said. "I mean, I never thought it was."

Mrs. Triton sighed. How could she share her sorrow with Natalie? Natalie had never been truly sorry.

Sidonie married a farmer in Oregon. She said she did not know how it happened.

○ ○
○

The afternoon Mr. Triton left the running of the world to others, his investments started to go bad. There was a fishing boat and there were girls, but they were all gone now. One day Mr. Triton was actually poor. He had to go live with a Mrs. H. Carmen. You won't end up on no park bench with me, honey, she told Mr. Triton. It wasn't too bad. But it was wine instead of Scotch.

What troubled Mrs. Triton was not that everything had slipped away but that she could accept its loss, adjust to all these changes. I'm free, she said when no one was around to hear.

She had always thought Natalie's husband too attractive for Natalie. So she called him, and Izzy was glad she did. He thought Mrs. Triton cute, petite, really his kind of dish.

"How rotten!" Natalie shouted. "How absolutely rotten! You are never to see Izzy again, do you hear?"

"I'll do as I wish," Mrs. Triton said.

There were sharp stones where they were fighting. The weight of Natalie on her neck made Mrs. Triton gasp. There were groans. There were weird, guttural sounds.

A man came running from somewhere. He grabbed Natalie by the collar and peeled her off.

"You're a witness!" Mrs. Triton said.

Sidonie had three children by the Oregon farmer. She was taking two correspondence courses from the state university. Sylvia had a job and a small apartment in L.A. Bird was somewhere too. Sandra had been placed with a man named Ralph. All the daughters kept in touch. But they never visited each other. They had so little in common since the years had first divided them. Once in a while they tried to locate their mother. But her number was unlisted, address guarded, Raven & Cross no longer her lawyers. Therefore they could not make her sad for them ever, ever again.

D Y S L E X I A

My mother swears I could recite the alphabet before I could walk. At the time I was in elementary school, the phonetic method was in the ascendancy. I was taught to sound out the vowels. Consonants were then added as prefixes whether or not they made sense. Thus, ba, be, bi, bo, bu. When these sounds were firmly known, consonants were added as suffixes. Thus, bat, bet, bit, bot, but. The system grew in complexity until even Mississippi was possible. But I do not know the actual moment when I could read or when I knew that I could.

Ramon suggests that I read *Manon Lescaut.* Impossible. I am sorely lacking in time. Have to finish *Age of Innocence* and all of James Fenimore Cooper. Must also buy for supper. Remember to pick up cleaning. Cleaners closes at six. I read Edith Wharton on the way.

Mother suggests de Maupassant. *A Woman's Life.* I am learning from these books, Mother says. The hard lot of a woman. Lives destroyed by men. Mother, I protest. It was you who left Father. Not the other way around. And you do not struggle. Inwardly, Mother says, and looks aggrieved. Promise to read de Maupassant. Gratified to note it is a short book. Read two chapters about Natty Bumppo. Am not a fan of pioneer life as idyll. Meeting re book tomorrow. Summer approaches. If possible, get someone to plant seeds. Garden has gone—um —to seed.

Ramon meets me at Burger King. Kisses me ardently in the fashion of the young. Asks me with onion breath what I thought of *Manon Lescaut.* Damn, I say. Halfway through *Deerslayer,* three chapters of *Age of Innocence,* and promised Mother before sleep to read de Maupassant. Not politic to mention Charles and *Life of Voltaire.* Burst into tears. There, Ramon consoles. I did not mean to scold. I will, Ramon, I whisper. I will start *Manon Lescaut* this very evening.

Professor Wheaton displeased with Leatherstocking report. Says my grasp of primitive hero is jaded. How can a grasp be jaded? Just bored with Natty Bumppo. Professor Wheaton stares at me. Good woolen sweater, flannel skirt, diamond-patterned stockings. Am I too clean? Come, Professor Whea-ton says. We go for coffee. The returning student faces unique problems, he says. He pats my hand. I gaze back with carefully arranged jaded expression. Professor Wheaton pulls book from book bag. Next meeting, he says. Read this. *The Rainbow.* Pay special attention to third chapter. Are you free for dinner? I shake head. Professor Wheaton understands and nods. Have seen him with wife and progeny in Washington Square. Another time, he insists.

Charles asks what I think of Voltaire. I roll from memory notes made in the library. I make room every three sentences for Charles to fill in. He does not notice when I stop altogether. Spaghetti, salad. Prop up *Age of Innocence* in plexiglass recipe-book holder. Newland Archer still indecisive.

Set alarm for five-fifteen. Will wash hair and blow dry in the morning. Look at Charles's sleeping back. He is truly tolerant of me. Open *A Woman's Life*. Adjust tensor lamp. Cannot skim. Mother shrewd and will know what's skipped. Jeanne and Julien. Read.

Notice on Wednesday that Charles is very interested in what Amalie Herring is saying. Sneak close on pretext of passing potato chips. Discussing *Volpone* and social satire. Overwhelmed with realization I am imperfect wife for Charles. Unable to share his interests. Will read *Volpone*.

Meet Ramon at Curly's loft. An ancient Stearns & Foster mattress on floor. Know brand because no sheets. Ramon already undressed. Ah, my love, he says. Only ten when I married Charles. Only eight when Morris Logan and I shared the back seat of his Chevrolet.

I drop my sweater and books. Hurry, my love, he says. Remove skirt, blouse, nylons. I do not have the hang of pantyhose. Ramon says exhilarating to see me unhook things.

Isn't *Manon* beautiful? I say nothing in reply. Exactly, Ramon says. Next you will read *Judith Paris*.

○　○
○

I peek at Charles's desk. He is reading *Body and Soul Together: Achieving the Welfare State*.

Professor Wheaton waves *The Rainbow* under my nose. Human relationships, he says. Who does Ursula make you think of? Sophia, Constance, May, the Widow Wadman? You, my dear, Professor Wheaton says. He has my hand. Caressing it, pressing it. How tired I am of the young, he says. How I long for a mature woman. Tell me, I beg, what is your opinion of Skrebensky? Should Ursula have studied more?

Your father, Mother says, wants me to have him back. On what terms? I ask. Terms, shmerms, my Mother says, the man cannot cope. Report on *Age of Innocence* declared to have "Greater wisdom and maturity than I am used to—Read for special paper *Death Comes for the Archbishop.*"

I guess you thought it was the suggestion of a schoolboy, my son Chester says. He touches *Tristam Shandy,* which is still on top of refrigerator, cover dusty. I was saving it for Thursday, I say. Immediately after dinner begin *Tristam Shandy.*

Barbara home from college. Is it true, she says archly, a student, my mother? Not full-fledged, I assure her. Just a few courses to get the feel. Unbelievable, she says. My mother. I wear a size nine dress, size seven shoes, and have hair that curls at will, up or down.

Barbara leaves house for rendezvous with old friends. Shamelessly plunder her suitcase. *Medieval Papacy, Collected Poetry of John Donne, College Outline of Biology.*

Your eyes are fine, Dr. Shapiro says. A little tired perhaps. Read by good light.

So how was *Tristam Shandy*? Chester says.

Amalie Herring pokes around secondhand book stores. She has bought Charles *A History of Italian Unity* (2 vols.), both volumes annotated by someone with a thick-nibbed pen. The handwriting is marvelous, she says. Look, Charles, she says.

It is a chante-fable, Ramon says. *Aucassin and Nicolette.* I myself have bought this just for you. With my pennies, my love. And why can't we be together when your husband goes to CPA convention? Because he is not a CPA, I say.

I have fallen asleep dreaming of Bishop Latour. Not necessary as it turns out. Professor Smelten has caught the flu. Caught it from Professor Wheaton's children when he had dinner in their West Village apartment.

No question Barbara taking the pill. Probably living with someone in California. May or may not be home this summer. Grades good. Not to worry, Charles says.

Headache. Left temporal lobe.

Losing myself in historical romances, Mother says. She's reading *Prisoner of Zenda*. Do you know that one? Must run. Meeting with Ramon. Don't forget cleaning, also bread.

Chester has a book for me. Paperback of *Mr. Britling Sees It Through*.

I am weeping with cheek against refrigerator door. Cleaning woman has broken vacuum. With broom sweep small Aubusson rug.

Dr. Shapiro tests for glasses. Pats hand comfortingly. Fine, all fine. Rest more. Relax.

Mother, Barbara says, I am afraid of biology.

But, Ramon asks, what did you *do* with yourself?

Graduated high school, married Charles. I did nothing with myself.

Wheaton skipping around. Please read *Marble Faun*. Have finished *Volpone*. Race to Charles with news. Has bemused expression in eyes. For what have I read *Volpone*? Ramon recommends *Marble Faun*. Letter from Barbara now back in school. Also copy of *Memoirs of a Midget*. Devoured in search of the apropos. Tensor lamp sizzles. Vacuum repaired. Cleaning woman made salad. Mother not taking Father back until he furnishes proof. Receive from Wheaton reading list, receive from Smelten ditto, receive from Ramon *Song of Bernadette*, receive from Charles *Remembrance of Things Past*, receive from Chester illustrated copy of *The Red Badge of Courage*, receive from Mother *The Sea Wolf*. Open any book. Kolod balejwaw pnimah nefesch jehudi homijah.

A WALKER'S
MANUAL

○ ○ ○ ○ ○

Whenever possible, I walk to my destination. In order to do
this, I must live at the very center of my activities. I am not
referring to walking as chore or as exercise but rather as
function, which, like breathing or drinking, cannot be stopped.
By constant walking, I have learned to use my hips and to
extend the length of my stride. Although I seem to be a fast
walker to those who move no more than from taxi to building,
I wear no speedometer and neither run nor jog. When it rains,
I ride, and I would never think of carrying heavy things in my
arms. In other words, I am not an obsessive walker, just a very
good one.

I feel sorry for those who do not walk and thus see the
world only from start to finish. Once, I joined a walking club
and rambled in the countryside. But the other walkers made
too much of it. They spoke of measured distances and of time,
and when they walked, it was a formal activity. They wagered
on endurance.

My only concession to scheduling is to map out my daily

rounds. It is inefficient to do otherwise. On the back of my kitchen door I have pinned a map with a red dot to represent my apartment house. Cross-streets for forty blocks in any direction are indicated. In ink, I have noted all the places where I might stop. Stores, theaters, homes of friends—a useful navigational scheme.

While walking, you have truly a chance to see. That is the pleasure of walking. The fifteenth-century monk Hegastus, who set himself walking as a penance, was horrified to discover how much he enjoyed the physical movement, how stimulating was the passing scene, men in fields, children at play. He prayed for guidance as his soles wore thin. He sent back letters intended for a pamphlet on the torment of walking. At last he bought shoes made by a poor craftsman. Calluses and bunions appeared. In bleeding pain and joy, he returned to the monastery.

My paternal grandmother, an Eastern European lady in whose custody I was often left, feared the intricacies of buses and subways. If you missed your stop on the subway, God knew where you would land. Once, holding tight to my hand, she took me on a subway. We were going in search of a freshly killed chicken in a store that might or might not be mythical. We missed our station, and when we ventured up the stairs to the street, it was to stand in an area of warehouses. As my grandmother muttered a prayer for our salvation, a car stopped across the street, and two men got out. One shot the other. The dead man fell face down. This is what happens when you don't know where you're going.

○ ○
○

My daughter Danielle does not walk, although she has hiked the Appalachian Trail and marched down into the Grand Canyon. She was the first in her group to have black patent slippers with T-straps. You cannot walk in such shoes. For children, it is best to buy brown leather oxfords, snub-nosed with a well-sewn welt. Christina of Sweden, in her romantic journey through New England, gave up pinching slippers for moccasins made of calfskin. A yielding shoe is the first necessity. A moccasin with padded sole provided Christina of Sweden with the perfect footwear to move through forest and along unpaved streets.

Walking leads to many pleasures. One afternoon in the suburbs, Georgette ran from her house and stood in the road wringing her hands. She offered me fifty dollars a week for life if I would never speak of the car that pulled into her driveway every afternoon at three. Of course, I took the money.

When you walk down a street, you look in windows, even into the windows of apartments or private residences if the blinds are up or the drapes are open. It was a miniature Queen Anne desk in the window of an antiques store that caught my attention, and I stopped. It was then that I saw them walking across the street. I had never seen her before.

She was young already, as I knew, early twenties, I'd say, slender and small and not unpretty. Her head just reached his shoulder. They weren't holding hands, but their arms swung together in an intimate rhythm. Occasionally their fingers clasped and unclasped. She wore a plaid coat and a small red tam. Rigidly, I faced the store window, grateful that the street was wide. I followed their disgusting progress in the reflections of glass. She walked at a pace presumably not naturally hers —this, I surmised, to keep up with him. Two short steps and then a little skip. She was what Danielle would call smart, stylish. She looked okay to me too.

I started forward, foolishly quickening my step until I felt the beat of my heart. It was inevitable that I should at some time or other see my former husband. No matter what else changes, habits remain—the same bakery, tailor, dimestore. Charmel, in his account of walking through England, speaks of meeting the same person first down one twist of the road and then again far away on another. Charmel, as best I can recall, does not mention his opinion of the people he thus encountered. My former husband, whom I have not seen for five years, a period long enough for wariness to dissolve, is not, however, someone I hold in high regard. We last met in the lawyer's office, divvying up the spoils.

I forced myself to complete my chores. I stopped in at the cleaners, where they were altering a skirt for me. Midcalf with a single pleat in the front. Too much material in a garment causes it to flap about the knees. It is tiring and interferes with movement. Slacks, of course, are perfect. They permit the stride unfettered. But skirts are once again in fashion and, being single, so must be I.

I carry paper bags in one hand and the box with the skirt in the other. Nigel said that the best time he had was strolling through Paris carrying nothing and buying nothing, a single key and two coins in his pocket.

The search for the perfect boot is difficult. It must protect the foot from the cold, yet remain light and supple. The boots that I already own are unsatisfactory. First of all, there is the question of appearance; those boots are thick and unshapely, suitable for suburban snowbanks. Friends tell me of a mail-order bootmaker in Maine, fearsomely expensive. I take the measurements that his advertisement requests and attach these to a cardboard tracing of my feet. The boots, ordered late, do not arrive until early December. When I open the package, the things within tremble. The leather softened with neat's-foot oil glows and glistens with life. I am transformed. The dreariness of winter is lifted.

I go forth again, my stride never better than it is. It is past two in the afternoon, and I am almost late for my two-twenty class in antiques. The school is twelve blocks away. After class, I stop in the midtown library for the books that I have reserved on dolls. In his heuristic account *Winter Walks*, LeGere says that in the wind one must remove one's head-covering and permit the hair to blow freely. The pleasure will make the cold as nothing. As I unfastened my scarf, they emerged from a restaurant hardly more than a cold breath away. He holds her arm as he escorts her to the edge of the curb. Then he turns up his collar against the weather and steps into the street to signal for a cab. She waits on the sidewalk, secure and confident. One thing he never had with me was trouble getting a taxi.

I was paralyzed. Nothing could have made my legs move past them. A taxi did a pas de deux through the traffic and slid to the curb. He opened the door and stood back for her to enter. She wore high boots made for curb-to-building travel. His hand touched her arm. I take care of you, the gesture said.

o o
o

Following Danielle's advice, I have my hair cut. It will be a while before I can adjust. Gusts no longer whip stray strands across my forehead as I walk. I have the giddy sensation of false Ménière's disease. As a child, I read an interview with the ingenue Sally Martin. She said that after her hair was bobbed she walked through the streets with the first liberty she had known in years.

Jake, a friend from college days, is giving a party at his Long Island estate. The waterfront paths permit one to walk for two unobstructed miles. I planned to go. Mr. Stanley would be my escort. I'd met him at an auction, where he bought a small wooden train and a doll I didn't want. Afterwards, we talked. I found him amusing and companionable enough. I bought a silver-gray chiffon dress, the merest froth of a garment, dips and panels and triangular sleeves. There are occasions, perhaps once or twice in your life, when you look supremely right, and the narcissistic impulse races forward. I caught glimpses of myself in every reflective object.

So I walked with Mr. Stanley through the summer night. Mr. Stanley was chilled. We returned to the house. As we sipped champagne in the second-floor ballroom, I saw them enter the hall. I was truly startled. Jake must know her. That must be it. I turned away, wondering if I dared suggest to my escort that we tour the grounds again. Her hair, as long as Danielle's, swung free. She wore silk pajamas with the color, the cut, the swagger of youth.

I decided that she looked unutterably out of place.

My attention turned to my foot. It hurt. It was the silver sandal, a concession to the dress. The next morning I could barely hobble. I went to my podiatrist. "Stay off your feet," he said.

○ ○
○

I have decided to have all my footwear made by hand. I begin to think about the last, about the instep, about interior construction and ventilation. These feet of mine must serve me till the end. On both sides of my family the women lived well into their eighties. The daughter of the King of Seville practically walked to her funeral.

I am walking down the west side of the street to avoid the direct heat of the sun. I see them waiting across the way for the light to change.

I have placed the key to my apartment on a chain around my neck and I have wrapped in tissue three one-dollar bills tucked into the single pocket of my cotton skirt. I have abandoned all synthetic materials for summer. Pure cotton absorbs perspiration and keeps the body cool. Unfortunately, I am sometimes recognized by residents and shopkeepers on certain streets. But I do not break my stride. I pretend to be winding my watch. Or I clutch my jaw in imaginary pain. People, the eighteenth-century philosopher Langer writes, do not understand an activity that is beyond their understanding.

U L C E R

List daily intake.

Spicy Szechuan beef shreds, braised kale with onions, salted almonds, *pommes de terre.* I pushed the forms away. Looked again at the checklist. The food on that list was all white. I had been eating it for days. It was soft, gelatinous, without form or aroma. Pick one choice from each group and put an *X* in the box. Carefully, I put *X*'s down the entire list. I am defying the diet that is intended to defy the operation.

You are a thin person, the doctor said, and consume little. But that little must be reoriented. He poked at my stomach. Else snip-snip.

What is your attitude toward food?

My parents were very active in the Socialist Party and in ORT and in other refugee organizations when I was a child. They were very foreign, never spoke more than minimal English, and did not value American customs, least of all the custom of privacy. There were always too many people in my house, some *landsleit,* but most strangers. There was perforce a communal kitchen. I was not a very attractive child, and I knew it. When an old man who came afternoons to sit in the kitchen and sip tea would pinch my cheek and whisper *"Schöne mädchen,"* I knew he lied. Ignored and basically less interesting than my brother, who had memorized whole passages from certain political pamphlets, I spent most of my time where the cooking was done. It was from the women in the kitchen that I learned. It is not to be thought for a moment that all was hearty peasant fare, although we did have our nights of black bread, onions, smetana. We also had soups of elegant subtlety, cassoulets intended for the rich, tortes silky with cream.

The ability to cook proved to be a distinct advantage. Furthermore, it made me happy. Cooking helped to develop the giving side of my nature. It made other people content and amiable. Doubtless, it was tied up with maternal deprivation. But still my *quenelles de veau* can vie with birdsong, and the great heat of my steak *au poivre* will melt the frostiest mood.

What is the relation of pain to food?

Darrell married me and bought me a home with a large kitchen, where I cooked and was very good for his law practice. People liked to come to dinner. I walked among my guests, smiled, asked them how they were. It is part of the largess of the food-giver.

Bertha and Winthrop were born and helped to grow sage and rosemary and chervil in the garden. Neither was much interested in cooking, but both grew up with sophisticated tastes and a knowledge of wine. Their friends liked to come over too. I always cook the right food for the right people.

Darrell is a devoted husband. I do not believe that he fools around. "Why should I go shopping when I live in a department store?" he said one night as he bit into a nutmeg sand tart.

Once, after a dinner party, a man followed me into the kitchen. It might have been Barney Rosenstock. Anyway, he looked around and shook his head. "So this is where you do it. I imagined shelves full of iridescent tinctures and clouds of colored gases."

There is no question but that I am an extraordinary cook. Who could blame Barney Rosenstock for noticing?

What part does food play in your social life?

There was never any help in the kitchen. I never hired anyone to serve. Therefore, after a dinner I usually had a few tasks to finish in the kitchen before rejoining my guests. Often, a man would come into the kitchen on the pretext of helping. It happened all the time. Full of good food and wine, they'd reach for me. But I knew how to manage them. "Hand me that," I'd say.

"I'm in great trouble in the office. I think they're on to me. If they check the Arc and Company account, I've had it," Charlie said.

"Hand me the mayonnaise," I said.

Underline the appropriate words.

burning	rhythmicity	scalding	lumpiness
tightness	irritation	strangulation	vacuity
wavy feeling	scorching	tickling	despond

Do the symptoms appear after eating?

When I was a young woman, everyone dressed neatly with Peter Pan collars. But they were too symmetrical for my irregular features.

Then one day ladies no longer wore Peter Pan collars. Everyone wanted to look interesting and different. I had wild hair and different features. And I could cook.

One Wednesday the water in a pot of potatoes boiled out. The singed potatoes welded themselves to the pot and sent serious smoke through to the second floor. I had to serve Florentine noodles with the lamb. It was the first burning.

On Thursday the Rosenstocks and the Byrds came to dinner. The gravy was sour. A gurgling noise started in my throat as, overcome with horror, I tasted it.

Half the night Darrell kept me up. What was wrong? I could explain nothing. I was neither tired nor menopausal. My life was moving along exactly as expected.

In steady, orderly procession disasters erupted at routine dinners and also at festive occasions. A charred ham. The same spice used twice. Something undersalted.

Bertha nibbled at a bit of chicken. "No flavor. Skin burned. Boy, this is the pits." She turned to her father. "If I get a job this summer, I'm moving out."

"Jeez," Winthrop said, "you know I hate baked apple. We all hate baked apple. How could you forget?"

The smell of scorched oil crept under the door and into the dining room. People sniffed cautiously. Darrell threw open a window.

Does eating alleviate the symptoms?

Charlotte Byrd came to see me. "It is time you were liberated," she said. "Your subconscious is telling you as much. You have been a slave to the demands of your family. Cooking, cooking, cooking. And for what? Why don't you get out in the world and become a caterer?"

Would you object to psychiatric counseling?

Color, taste, and appearance, they are all crucial in food. And, of course, there is aroma. "It stinks." Bertha wrinkled her nose. "Smells like a thousand cloves of vomit."

"Are you having an affair?" Darrell asked after dinner.

I sought professional help. Dr. Wesco was very reassuring. It was a common malady. I was a middle-aged lady. Life had swept away from me. Naturally, I felt a certain loss, a certain stress. He was certain I could learn to handle it. I had only to attend to my own needs.

I signed up for a series of modern dance lessons. I planned an entire program of menus around my favorite food.

Dr. Wesco sedated me. Overwork, exhaustion, modern times.

I went back into the kitchen renewed. I made tiny meatballs fragrant with garlic and basil snipped fresh from my herb garden. I put up spaghetti and set the timer for *al dente* and checked it with my watch. I made a salad and chopped dill. The meatballs simmered on the stove. It was then that I saw movement from either near the broom closet or the door that led to the basement. The hand that shot out was swift.

It turned a knob so that the tomato sauce boiled.

I had seen it. I had seen the hand. It was someone turning up the flame, someone turning up the oven, someone switching spices.

I took down my meal-planner notebook. I sought out an empty page and began a sketch. I would redesign the kitchen. I would create a work island in the middle of the floor. I would surround myself with lots of space. Barney Rosenstock could come stand with me in it.

Who does the cooking in your family?

Me. The power is immense.

THE PERSON
WHO HELD THE
○ JOB BEFORE YOU ○

Everyone had assembled in the conference room to wait for the
meeting to begin. They stood in groups of two and three around
the coffee urn and the pile of Danish. It was Monday, so there
was talk that had nothing to do with work. The conference
room was just a conference room—gray tile floor, green metal
table, orange plastic chairs with chrome legs. Stacks of multi-
lithed forms stood at one end of the table.

The first sounds were clear and distinct. They caused startled reactions. Waves of coffee splashed to cardboard edges.
White frosting got stuck on lips.

The voice came through the wall or through the air vent.
Loud and clear, the woman called, "Help! Help!" Over and
over.

Everyone stopped talking. The men did not look at each
other.

They were not brave. The women could not be expected
to go to a rescue. But they could be expected to be annoyed.

"What is it?" they asked, looking at each other and at the

men, who did not look back. "Who is calling? Is it the P.A. system?"

"Next door," one of the men said, and hated himself for saying it—for it singled him out.

"Next door?" a woman repeated. "That's Mrs. Casso. Isn't that Mrs. Casso next door?"

They all looked at the man who had spoken.

The woman next door kept calling. She kept calling, "Help! Help!"

"For God's sake," the women said. "Do something!"

The man who had called attention to himself felt the terrible pressure.

"Come on," he said hoarsely. "Let's go."

One of the women opened the door. The men moved with military spirit into the hall.

The door next door was identical. One man tried to turn the knob.

"Mrs. Casso!" everybody called.

They heard the woman shriek, "Help! Help!"

One of the women pulled a key ring from her purse. "Here is a master key," she said.

The others looked at her. It had not been previously known that this woman was important enough to have a key of any kind.

The man who had called attention to himself put the key into the lock and turned it. He could feel the quickened beat of his heart. His palms were damp. He turned the doorknob, released the catch, and then abruptly kicked the door open, leaving a footprint on the wood.

Everyone jumped back, those in front pushing into the soft bodies of those behind.

Mrs. Casso sat on a vinyl chair. It was the standard office chair. Her arms hung at her sides. Her office was very neat, the piles of papers squared off.

"Help! Help!" Mrs. Casso said.

Slowly, the men moved into the office. They examined Mrs. Casso.

"What is it?" someone from the back who could not see called out. "Is she tied up?"

The woman who had the master key pushed herself forward. "Mrs. Casso," she said. "Have you been attacked?"

Mrs. Casso's hair was combed, clothes in no way disturbed. "Help! Help!" she cried.

"Stop it," the woman with the master key said.

"Help! Help!"

What do we do? Everyone looked at each other. They were at loss.

"We'll have to call someone," said the man who had kicked open the door.

Someone took a copy of the office phone book from the top of Mrs. Casso's desk. Printed on the inside cover were the numbers for Police, Fire, Security.

"That's it," the woman said. She leaned across Mrs. Casso and from habit said, "Excuse me," as she picked up the phone.

Was there contagion on this phone? Tonight she must remember to gargle.

Security was comforting. "Don't worry," a voice said. It was a voice worldly in the ways that were rough. "Hang on," Security said. "We'll call for assistance."

"Help! Help!" said Mrs. Casso.

"You've been in analysis, Alfred," someone said. "Is Mrs. Casso in a trance?"

"Haven't the faintest," Alfred said.

"No meeting today," a man said.

They all stayed with Mrs. Casso. It was easy now. She just sat there calling, "Help! Help!"

From the elevator come two men in white coats. They are grinning. But when they see the people congregated in the hall, they become solemn and businesslike.

"What's up?" one man says.

"Help! Help!" Mrs. Casso says.

"Stand back, folks," the other man says.

The two men enter the room where Mrs. Casso sits. They enter crouching, their long arms reaching in front of them.

"Is she dangerous?" one man says.

"Nonsense," says the woman with the master key. "Mrs. Casso is Accounts."

Each man grips one of Mrs. Casso's arms. Mrs. Casso does not resist. They assist Mrs. Casso onto the stretcher. They unfurl a sheet over Mrs. Casso. Over the sheet they buckle straps that buckle Mrs. Casso down.

"We are taking her to the city hospital for this zip code," the men say.

"What now?" someone says.

"Notify the family," someone else suggests. "And call Personnel."

So they called Personnel. That's how you got the job.

A FAMILY
HISTORY

O O O O O

I know three people who have committed suicide. I think that
it is unusual to know three people who have done this. They
did it in conventional ways and for the usual reasons. They did
not know each other. They left behind scheduled lives and
unkept appointments. People gathered in small groups after
the news and sieved from their memories bits of information.

Now every morning I examine my face.

It is no one's business.

There was one drowning, one shooting, one overdose of
drugs.

As a result of this, I have become very introspective. I
think about continuity. Sometimes, I turn to my husband and
say, What shall I do with my jewelry? For goodness sakes, he
replies.

My jewelry is in a small mahogany chest, a reproduction
of a sixteenth-century casket. In it are the pieces my husband
gave me. He knows I am not referring to those. I mean the gold
chain my father purchased for my mother in 1910. There is
also a bracelet that belonged to my great-grandmother. It was

given to her by an Austrian Horse Guard as a pledge of love before she was sent to America. There are three silver filigree pins that I can trace back to a great-great-grandmother. And even a lavaliere whose history is not gone.

There will be no deathbed scene with my two daughters gathered round as I solemnly hand over the casket. Our oldest daughter left in the great exodus of children. Let her go, my husband said, although once we wired money to Arizona. Ann, who is our youngest and who for a time was quite difficult, has gone to live on a farm near Rochester. She studies Oriental philosophies and proselytizes us with long letters. But she does not answer the questions in mine.

My daughters never wanted to know about my childhood, and I have lost the opportunity to tell them their family history as told to me by my mother and to which I have added my own observations.

○ ○
○

We had cousins who lived on the east side of town. Cissie, who was the oldest of the two sisters, changed her named to Sylvana. She became a flamenco dancer. There is an oil painting of her in the City Art Museum. She is draped with a black shawl embroidered with blue and gold camellias and is immortalized in a pivotal pose. When I was in high school, I took three friends to see this picture. But all the title said was "Dancer." I knew who she was. But they only hooted. I later searched for some snapshot of Sylvana, to link her to the painting—but there were only a few views of her as a child. After all, she had run away from home at fourteen.

The other two cousins were Joseph and Paulette. Joseph was the oldest. He was mostly called R.R., because that was the name of the chain of stores he owned. He had six of them, from St. Louis to Carbondale. Paulette and her brother lived in four rooms in a building R.R. owned. You would not believe that they had money. Paulette did all the cleaning and cooking. She was always dressed in black and had frizzy hair. Sylvana had the beauty, and R.R. had the money.

Find her someone, the family begged R.R. A man in your position.

R.R. seemed to pay no attention. But then one day he turned up with a man named Mochele. A young man, not handsome but presentable, a bit pudgy and nervous. R.R. brought him home to dinner. Paulette made chicken and dumplings and cherry strudel. Her dress was open at the neck, revealing white skin. She seemed, after all, vulnerable and touching.

Mochele came to dinner three or four times a week. R.R. stayed in the kitchen. If you came to visit during those times, R.R. made you sit with him in the kitchen and whisper.

How is it going?

Love birds, R.R. would say, winking. Just a pair of love birds.

R.R. announced the wedding. Simple, he said. An aging bride in white looks like a fool. A simple little wedding in the rental hall down the street that he could get for a song, a simple little supper catered by a very good buy.

The bride did not look good. Her hair had been badly arranged. The dress was a poor choice. Still, there was a serenity about the face, a certain relaxation.

After the ceremony, when everyone was gathered around the buffet table, Mochele and R.R. went into the little entrance-way.

Well, Mochele said, I married her, now where's the check?

R.R. only smiled.

Mochele moved his fingers in his nervous way. Where's the money?

R.R. smiled.

I'll leave, Mochele said. I swear.

Paulette stood there in the doorway, jaw getting slack.

Pay, Paulette said.

o o
 o

Vynella took me to the apartment. The place was scented with the odors of food. Not offensive though, none of your grease of today. But rather the fragrance of roasting fowl, simmering fruit, a *tzimmes* turning brown.

It's for rent, Vynella says, and not bad for the space and considering it faces front.

True, I say, appearing to be considering the rooms. I measure them off with my feet.

A woman died here, Vynella says. Maybe ten, twelve years ago. She starved to death. They found her sitting cross-legged, stiff as a board.

I myself would rather be dead than end up an old woman who died unmourned.

No, Vynella says. It wasn't like that at all. She was young. I remember her. We lived across the street in those days. She starved to death on purpose. She had some kind of belief, Vynella says, frowning and trying to remember. Starved to death *deliberately*, she says. Nice-looking woman, too.

I decided on the spot to take the apartment. Where can you find a place with a legend?

o o
o

Vynella was engaged to marry the Settleman boy when he was twenty-two. A pale, hothouse boy destined, as were all boys of his time, to do great things in the world. I remember the engagement as a time of extreme pain, Mrs. Settleman threatening to sit in mourning. But Vynella's family was rich, and the Settlemans were mere workers. Despite strong pressure from Mrs. Settleman, the engagement was announced.

But as the wedding day approached, Vynella became nervous and lost weight. The sight of a broken mirror or of a black cat threw her into hysterics.

Ira, she begged the Settleman boy, we must run away and be married. We must not wait.

But Ira was not a total dreamer. If they ran away, then the gifts, the money, the plans would all be forsaken.

Nothing will happen, he assured Vynella. Nothing.

Vynella grew thinner and more morose. The Settleman boy could stand it no longer.

We'll go to Chicago on Friday, he told Vynella. I have made arrangements. We will be married. But no one will know. And we will catch an afternoon train home. On Sunday, we will have the wedding as planned.

Oh, Ira, Vynella said.

They were married by a judge in Chicago. Vynella wore a suit. The judge brought in two men to be witnesses.

At the conclusion of the ceremony, one of the witnesses

went up to the Settleman boy. I've been trying to place you, he said. Your face was so familiar, and then it came to me. I don't know you, but I know your father.

My God, the Settleman boy said.

Vynella turned away and began to weep. The Settleman boy walked away with the man. Please, he begged. Don't tell anyone. We plan to return home this very afternoon. Sunday, there will be a wedding, a ceremony of the proper kind.

The man frowned. I don't know, he said. I can't give my word.

o   o
o

Selena, one hand dramatically gripping the front of her pink silk suit, dropped dead in a café on the Piazza dei something. Champleon stared with disbelief as his wife collapsed to the floor. The young man with whom they'd been eating immediately vanished. Champleon found that his knowledge of Italian was not sufficient to handle the situation.

A Selena alive and with passport in hand was moved easily from place to place. But dead, Selena was a terrible burden. There were forms to be filled out, officials who must seek other officials whose command of English was better. All Champleon wanted was to return his wife to the United States for burial. His shirts, his suits ran black with sweat as he attempted to perform this duty.

Selena was cremated. Champleon's married daughter came from Topeka for the ceremony. Afterwards, Champleon told her that he could manage just fine from here. The daughter was much relieved and flew home. Shortly thereafter, so did Champleon.

Since I had missed the funeral of Cousin Selena, I drove to Philadelphia to see Champleon. I arrived about four in the afternoon. Champleon greeted me in his large, comfortable living room.

Sherry? he said.

I'd really rather have something stronger, I said.

Good, he said, so would I.

By early evening, we had finished the bottle.

I'm glad, I said, that you are taking it so well.

Did you know, Champleon said, that she left me a large sum of money?

No, I said. But she was very astute. I always guessed as much.

She was a blackmailer, he said. She actually blackmailed people.

And she was successful? I said.

My God, he said. But don't you understand? That's where all the money came from. I mean I never put two and two together.

Well, I said, she couldn't actually have been overburdening anyone, or else there would have been trouble.

There's a safe deposit box, he said. Files, records, initials, codes.

What'll you do with it?

Burn it, he said.

Better wait, I said. Don't be in such a hurry.

What do you mean? It's evidence. Are you crazy? he said.

Then burn it, I said. If it will give you peace.

Yes, he said. Right, right. Yet I wonder, though. The people she blackmailed—I mean, she must have known something about them that they didn't want known.

Yes, of course, I said.

Yes, he said. But how do you figure she found it out?

○ ○
○

R.R. was dead. At my mother's request, I flew home from California for the funeral. I was told that I was mentioned in the will. As it turned out, I was bequeathed a set of leather-bound volumes, a complete set of the Boone County survey reports for 1874.

R.R. lay in a mahogany casket with a slumber lining of blue silk. Paulette stood near a wall. She greeted people with considerable grace. Her black suit was notably chic. It had been at least fifteen years since I'd last seen her. She was slender, and her hair was strikingly styled. She smoked and laughed and shook hands, and sometimes she inclined her head and touched cheeks.

○ ○
○

It was intended that these be told at campfires or on summer evenings on screened porches alive with creaking wooden boards. But there are no creakings any more and summer evenings stopped happening so long ago. If the time should come when I am ready for suicide, in the parting note that is required I would say good-bye, saddened by nothing save the absence of anyone to address it to.